CRASH LANDING!

"I'm going to take us higher!" George called, raising his voice over the roar of the engine. As the tiny plane began to climb, George looked more relaxed. He forgot all his cares when he was flying.

Hey, he thought suddenly, his heart skipping a beat as the yoke stopped vibrating in his hand. *Something's wrong!*

"What is it?" Enid yelled. But she didn't have to raise her voice. The cockpit had suddenly become very quiet.

"BA329 to Air Traffic Control," George said quickly into the radio. "My engine's cut out, and I've got no power. Can you read me?"

"This is Air Traffic Control," a voice announced. "BA329, are you sure you can't get any function from your engine?"

"I'm sure," George answered. Then the plane started to plummet, and Enid, bracing herself with both hands against the control panel, began to scream.

Bantam Books in the Sweet Valley High Series
Ask your bookseller for the books you have missed

SWEET VALLEY HIGH

CRASH LANDING!

Written by
Kate William

Created by
FRANCINE PASCAL

BANTAM BOOKS
TORONTO • NEW YORK • LONDON • SYDNEY • AUCKLAND

RL 6, IL age 12 and up

CRASH LANDING
A Bantam Book / June 1985

Sweet Valley High is a trademark of Francine Pascal

Conceived by Francine Pascal

Produced by Cloverdale Press Inc.
133 Fifth Avenue, New York, N.Y. 10003

Cover art by James Mathewuse.

ISBN 0-553-24947-9

Published simultaneously in the United States and Canada

Bantam Books are published by Bantam Books, Inc. Its trademark, consisting
of the words "Bantam Books" and the portrayal of a rooster, is Registered in
U.S. Patent and Trademark Office and in other countries. Marca Registrada.
Bantam Books, Inc., 666 Fifth Avenue, New York, New York 10103.

PRINTED IN THE UNITED STATES OF AMERICA

O   15   14   13   12   11   10   9   8   7   6

CRASH LANDING!

One

"I can't believe how beautiful it is up here!" Enid Rollins exclaimed, looking down through the window of the tiny plane at the rolling green hills surrounding Secca Lake.

George Warren glanced anxiously at Enid and sighed as he pulled back on the yoke, gently turning the two-seater Cessna 150 through the cloudless sky. He wished he could share Enid's delight. Despite the joy flying gave him, he couldn't suppress his growing uneasiness. Not about the plane—ever since he was a little boy George had longed to be a pilot, and now that he had his pilot's license, his dream was partly fulfilled. No, it wasn't flying that was making George uneasy. It was Enid. *Today's the day*, he thought resolutely. *No matter how awful it is to do it, I've got to tell Enid about Robin and me.*

One glance at Enid told George that this wasn't the right moment. Her green eyes were dancing with excitement, and her face was flushed with the thrill of this afternoon's adventure. "George, thank you so much for letting me come up here with you," she said suddenly, turning to him and smiling warmly. "It means so much to me that I'm the first person you've taken up!"

"A promise is a promise." George sighed as he turned the yoke to the right to guide the plane gently around the curve of the lake below. *Poor Enid*, he thought sadly. *She has no idea how I feel. If only there were some way I could have kept myself from falling in love with Robin.*

Robin Wilson. Just thinking about her made George's heartbeat quicken. But shame flooded through him as he realized that he'd been thinking about Robin while Enid was talking to him. How could he do this to Enid? They'd known each other for ages—years and years, although they hadn't seen each other during most of the time he'd been in boarding school. But since last fall, they'd been boyfriend and girlfriend. George had looked Enid up when he'd come home to Sweet Valley on vacation from school. He had found her even more wonderful than he'd remembered—a little quieter, maybe, and more studious. But she was as pretty as ever with her curly, shoulder-length brown hair and gentle smile.

George had graduated midyear from boarding school and had immediately enrolled at Sweet Valley College. He and Enid saw each other as much as possible.

Yes, George admitted to himself, lifting the plane's nose as they climbed above the hills, the two of them had been through a lot together. Not only had he loved her, but also she'd been the best friend he'd ever had.

In fact his affection for Enid had kept him from admitting what was happening between Robin and him for a long time. George had known Robin Wilson for some time now. She was at most of the parties he'd gone to with Enid, and he'd always thought she was both pretty and a nice person. But she was a friend of Enid's, one of her classmates, and nothing more to him. It wasn't until they starting spending time together in flying class that things began to change. George had never met anyone like Robin before. They had so much in common. He could tell her everything. Her passion for planes and flying was as great as his; she was the first girl who'd ever understood his dream of becoming a pilot.

At first George had refused to admit that the feelings he had for Robin were growing beyond casual friendship. When he *did* realize what was happening, he tried his hardest to stop it. He left flight class early so he wouldn't be able to talk to Robin at all. He avoided her eager smile and made excuses when she asked him for help on take-home preparation material. But when they were paired on their first flying assignment, George knew it was all over. He had fallen in love, and there was nothing he could do about it.

George and Robin had talked the whole thing

3

out. It hadn't been easy for Robin, either. She had been torn between loyalty to Allen Walters, her steady boyfriend, and her growing affection for George. But the first time George took Robin in his arms they both knew they'd been fooling themselves. This was love, real love. And no matter how badly it hurt Enid and Allen, they would have to be told.

Earlier, at the awards ceremony marking the end of their flight class, Robin had looked terribly upset. "I told Allen," she had whispered to George. "It was terrible, but I'm glad he knows the truth. I couldn't stand deceiving him for another minute."

And now it's my turn, George thought sadly, pulling the throttle out as he swooped the plane low over the lake. He and Robin had decided that the last day of their flying class would be the cut-off point. *But he had promised Enid he'd take her flying, and he wanted to keep that promise before telling her.*

"Hey, look!" Enid exclaimed, peering down at the sandy beach edging Secca Lake. "I can see people down there. I wonder if anyone from Sweet Valley High is watching us!"

George bit his lip. He had a feeling Robin was watching from the shore. She knew that he was taking Enid up over the lake in a rental plane that afternoon, and he was sure she was down below now, watching them. *Which makes everything even worse,* he thought miserably.

"Do you think they're watching us?" Enid

asked, leaning as far forward as her safety harness would allow. The people down at the lake looked like tiny specks of color from so high up.

"Who cares?" George answered, more vehemently than he'd meant to. He pulled back gradually on the yoke, bringing the nose of the Cessna up.

"What are you doing?" Enid cried, her eyes sparkling with excitement.

"I'm going to take us higher!" George called, raising his voice over the roar of the engine. As the tiny plane began to climb, George looked more relaxed. He forgot all his cares when he was flying. It was so peaceful up there, he told himself, and the plane was so easy to maneuver. All he had to do was touch the yoke, and it responded perfectly, George thought. Up there—

Hey, he thought suddenly, his heart skipping a beat as the yoke stopped vibrating in his hand. *Something's wrong!*

"What is it?" Enid yelled. But she didn't have to raise her voice. The cockpit of the tiny plane had suddenly become very quiet.

"The engine," George told her, gritting his teeth as he tried desperately to get it started again. "It's cut out."

"BA329 to Air Traffic Control," George said quickly into the radio. "Can you read me? We're having trouble up here. The engine's cut out, and I've got no power. Can you read me?"

"This is Air Traffic Control," a voice

announced. "BA329, are you sure you can't get any function from your engine?"

"I'm sure," George answered. The Cessna was beginning to plummet, and Enid, bracing herself with both hands against the control panel, began to scream.

"Have you got a clearing?" Air Traffic Control demanded.

His heart beating wildly, George scanned the landscape beneath him. "Only the lake," he shouted. "Secca Lake. We're falling fast!"

"Get the nose up!" Air Traffic Control urged him. "Face into the wind and take her down into the lake."

George had never been so frightened in his life. He had been told over and over again in his flight class what to do in a situation like this, but it sure felt different from up here. He knew a Cessna 150 would fall at the rate of about 750 feet a minute. To slow the descent he had to get the plane's nose up and turn her around into the wind. Then the tiny plane would glide into the water rather than crash straight down.

"I'm so frightened, George," Enid wailed. "What's happening? What are we going to do?"

George was frantically scanning the lake below to determine which way the wind was blowing. At last he was able to make out the ripples on the water's surface, indicating the wind was coming from the east. With all his might George moved the yoke. *Turn her around*, he prayed silently. *Please, God, turn her around.*

Unless he could turn the plane into the wind, George knew he and Enid were doomed. The plane would fall faster and faster without the wind to break their speed, and the impact of the crash would kill them.

"We're turning!" Enid screamed.

"Thank God." George sobbed, gripping the yoke with both hands. "Air Traffic Control," he gasped into the radio, "I've got us pointing due east, into the wind. We're in a nose-high attitude, heading for Secca Lake. Do you read me?"

"Keep her steady," Air Traffic Control advised.

"Enid," George said, panting and reaching out to steady her trembling shoulders, "the wind is going to help break our fall. We're going to attempt a crash landing into the lake, but remember—"

The blue water of Secca Lake seemed to be rising closer and closer beneath them.

"Remember what?" Enid screamed, closing her eyes.

"Open your door before we hit the water," George yelled over the rising rush of the wind. "Otherwise, it might jam shut. OK?"

"OK," Enid yelled back, tears coursing down her cheeks.

"Are you ready?" George screamed.

Enid took a deep breath. "Ready!"

"Now!" George hollered. "Get the door open because we're coming down!"

His words were drowned out as the tiny plane

hit the water. George felt nothing more than the shock of water spraying up around them. He was thrown forward against the windshield, and everything went dark and silent.

Enid, screaming so loud her throat ached, felt a sickening sensation in her stomach as the plane bounced once on the surface of the lake and flipped over.

It took a minute for Enid to figure out what had happened. The plane was floating upside down in the middle of the lake, buoyed by the light wings, so that the cockpit sat above the water like a small dome. At first Enid was so shaken she couldn't bring herself to open her eyes. But the next minute she heard something that made her eyes fly open in horror.

It was the sound of water lapping against the cockpit.

Enid couldn't believe what she saw when she looked around her. She and George were still strapped into their seats, hanging upside down in the tiny cockpit. It was like being in a ride in an amusement park. Her head was hanging several inches above the water, and the only thing keeping her from dropping down was the safety harness. "George!" Enid sobbed, trying to twist herself sideways so she could get a good look at him. Her neck hurt a little, but otherwise she was fine.

But George wasn't. Enid saw that at once. The impact of the crash had forced his seat forward, and he had been knocked out when his head had hit the windshield. Enid could see a jagged cut across his forehead. He was bleeding, but she couldn't see how badly.

But Enid knew he was alive. She wriggled her hand across him up to his mouth and nose and felt the warmth of his breath as he exhaled. *Thank God*, Enid thought. *Thank God he's alive*.

Enid's relief was short-lived. The plane was sinking slowly, and she knew it was only a matter of minutes before the cockpit filled completely. *We've got to get out of here*, she thought frantically, trying in vain to shake George into consciousness. She thought that if she released herself, she'd have a better chance to help George. Her fingers felt unbelievably clumsy as she fumbled with the straps of her harness. At last she managed to undo the buckle, and holding onto the strap with both hands, she lowered herself into the water at the bottom of the cockpit.

"George!" she cried, trying to reach up across him to unfasten his harness. But the cockpit was too narrow, and the buckle holding George prisoner in his seat was impossible to reach from that angle. "I'll have to get it from the other side," Enid muttered. Without stopping to think, she pushed the door open on her side of the cockpit and jumped into the cool water of the lake.

Everything Enid had learned in her junior lifesaving class the previous summer came back at once. The lake water made her clothing feel as heavy as lead, and in a flash she pulled off her cardigan sweater and kicked her loafers off her feet. Panting with exertion, Enid swam around the back of the plane to approach George's side of the cockpit. She could feel the blood pounding in her temples as she tried to pull herself up onto the underside of the wing. "Damn!" she cried, falling back into the water. It looked as though the cockpit had sunk even lower since she'd jumped into the lake; she could see the water touching George's forehead now. *I've got to save him,* she thought frantically.

The next minute Enid managed to pull herself up on the wing of the plane. Her wet socks didn't make it any easier to move across the metal wing, but she didn't have time now to take them off. She had to get George out of the plane, and she didn't have more than a minute or two left.

Leaning against the metal strut that attached the wing to the bottom of the cockpit, Enid put one arm around George's upper body while she snapped the buckle open with her left hand. The next instant George fell free of his harness, knocking Enid backward as he fell face first into the water.

The small of her back hit the metal strut hard, and Enid sucked in her breath as a dreadful pain shot up her spine. The next thing she knew, she had slid off the wet wing into the water. It felt as if her entire lower body had turned to lead, and she tried to balance herself on the wing so she wouldn't go under. *Something's wrong with me,* she thought desperately as the wing sank beneath her.

She had freed George just in time. Struggling to keep herself afloat, Enid saw the little plane bob once or twice before it sank.

"George!" Enid cried, pushing the strands of wet hair from her eyes as she tried to swim toward him.

"Don't move. I'm coming!" George called. The shock of the cool water had brought him back to consciousness, and within seconds he was at Enid's side.

"Thank God you're all right," Enid sobbed. "I was so frightened." Trying to stay afloat, she put her arms around George's neck. Something was wrong with her legs. She couldn't feel anything in either of them, and she couldn't seem to move them. Without George to hold her up, Enid was afraid she'd drown.

"What is it?" George gasped. "Are you hurt?"

Tears flowed down Enid's cheeks. "There's something wrong with my legs," she told him. "I can't seem to move."

George paled, tightening his arm around her. "Don't try to," he said urgently. "Just keep still. I'll get you to shore."

"George, I'm so frightened," Enid sobbed, gripping his arm as he began swimming.

"It's all right," George said. "It looks like a rescue team is coming out here! Are you in pain, Enid?"

Enid shook her head, her face ghostly pale. "I

can't feel a thing," she whispered. "George, I've lost all feeling in my legs!"

Todd Wilkins barely had time to think when he saw the little plane falter over Secca Lake. The handsome, brown-haired junior had been kicking a soccer ball around with Roger Patman and Ken Matthews when he heard a piercing scream from the shore. It was Robin Wilson, her face white as a sheet, her fumbling hand pointing at the sky. Shading his eyes with one hand, Todd had spotted the plane instantly. And he knew it was in trouble.

He ran as fast as he could to Secca Lodge, a shingled outbuilding that served as a changing house and refreshment stand several hundred yards from the lake. "Get me the police," he panted into the receiver of the pay phone inside. "Please," he added, his breath rasping. "It's an emergency!"

"Thanks, son," the officer had said when Todd had reported what he'd seen. "Air Traffic Control just notified us. There are three squad cars and an ambulance on the way."

The carefree picnic Todd had been enjoying with several of his classmates had been disrupted by the time he got back to the shore. Two or three groups from Sweet Valley High had had the same idea for an outing at the lake, and by now all were huddled together in the shallow water at the lake's edge, watching the Secca Lake

Emergency squad's boat motoring out to the sinking plane.

"Oh, Todd, it was awful," Olivia Davidson murmured, leaning against her boyfriend Roger Patman for support. "You should've seen the plane hit the water!"

"Is there anything we can do?" Todd asked helplessly.

Roger shook his head. "The squad asked us to stay out of the way," he said. "We can't do much now but wait."

"Does anyone know what happened to the people in the plane?" Todd continued, worried.

"We don't know yet," Ken Matthews said soberly. "But it's not just people, Todd. According to Robin Wilson it's George Warren and Enid Rollins."

"Oh, God," Todd murmured, spinning back to scan the lake for the emergency squad's white motorboat. George and Enid! It was impossible! He'd never dreamed the doomed plane was carrying friends.

Over the school year Todd had become good friends with both George and Enid. George was an excellent guy—great at sports, a good sense of humor—an all-around nice person. And Enid! Aside from being one of the best-tempered, most decent girls Todd had ever met, Enid was the best friend of his girlfriend, Elizabeth Wakefield. Through Elizabeth he'd gotten to know both George and Enid well. And now—

What if the rescue squad got there too late? Todd thought anxiously. What if—

"George!" a voice beside Todd called piteously. He turned. Robin Wilson, her brown eyes sparkling with tears, was standing next to him.

"They'll be OK," Todd said, hoping he sounded convincing. Robin was extremely agitated. He turned and looked out again across the lake and spotted the rescue boat heading toward shore. "They're in the back, Robin!" he said excitedly. "They've found them both."

"OK, kids, clear the way," one of the squad men said gruffly as the motorboat pulled up to shore. Todd couldn't remember when the ambulance had pulled up behind the small crowd on the shore, but it was there now, the red bubble on top spinning eerie glints of light onto the sand.

"Get a stretcher!" the squad man yelled, and the next minute the ambulance crew was racing forward. Todd realized he was trembling as he saw Enid being lifted carefully out of the boat onto the stretcher. Yes, she was alive, but she looked so pale, so helpless! Todd's heart went out to her.

"We need another stretcher!" a man from the ambulance squad called. A second stretcher was brought to the boat, and George was lifted onto it carefully. Todd saw that George, too, was alive, but clearly hurt. The paramedic wrapped his head in white gauze, but within seconds it was stained bright red with blood.

"George," Robin whispered, putting her hand up to her throat. "George."

"Hey," Olivia said suddenly, grabbing Roger's hand, "I think something's wrong with Robin. She looks awfully pale!"

Robin *had* gone pale. In fact, as the crew lifted George into the back of the ambulance beside Enid and turned on the siren, Robin Wilson fainted.

Two

"Mom, Enid's in that plane!" Elizabeth Wakefield burst out, her blue-green eyes wide with horror. "She might be in terrible danger!"

"I'll die if anything happens to Enid!" Jessica exclaimed, putting her arms around her twin.

Clutching each other in the dim interior of the Sweet Valley Police Station, Elizabeth and Jessica looked like mirror images. Blond, slim, and aqua-eyed, the twins were completely different despite their identical looks. But right now it was hard to tell that Elizabeth was usually calm and controlled, while Jessica tended to fly off the handle. Elizabeth was trembling all over, her eyes on the radio by Sergeant Malone's desk. "Please let them be all right," she said. "Please don't let anything happen to Enid!"

"Oh, no." Alice Wakefield, the twins' mother, moaned. "This can't be happening!"

"It looks like our ordeal isn't over at all," Ned Wakefield said with a sigh. The twins' father, a lawyer, often joked that crises were an everyday occurrence for him. But that day had been a little too much, even for him. The entire Wakefield family, with the exception of Steven, the twins' older brother, who was off at college, had gathered in the police station to fill out a report that Jack Howard, the boy Jessica had been dating, threatened her life.

Jessica was notorious for getting herself into trouble, but this time the Wakefields had been given a serious scare. The boy she'd been dating turned out to be a liar and a thief, as well as a drug user. When Jessica had found drugs in his apartment while she was visiting him, he'd suddenly turned violent. If Elizabeth and Nicholas Morrow, a friend of hers, and David Matson, an acquaintance of Nicholas's, hadn't turned up in time . . .

Twenty minutes before it looked as if their ordeal was over. Nicholas, David, and Elizabeth had been congratulated for their heroism, and Mr. and Mrs. Wakefield had announced that a celebration dinner was in order. But once the alert from Air Traffic Control had come through the radio on Sergeant Malone's desk, all thoughts of dinner were erased.

"Sergeant Malone?" the radio on the sergeant's desk cracked. "This is squad car five-five-six. We're at the scene of the accident. We've picked up two passengers, but the plane is lost."

Sergeant Malone looked quickly at the twins' frantic expressions and spoke into the radio receiver. "What's the condition of the passengers?"

"They're alive," the voice in the radio answered shortly. "We're sending them to Fowler Memorial Hospital in an ambulance right now. I can't say anything for sure about their condition."

"They're alive!" Elizabeth sobbed, throwing her arms around Jessica and holding her tightly. "Oh, Jess," she continued, wiping the tears from her face, "what if they're really hurt? Do you think Enid's OK?"

"What I think," Mr. Wakefield said firmly, slipping his arms around his daughters, "is that we'd better go to the hospital and see what we can find out. OK?"

Elizabeth took a deep breath, her lower lip quivering. "Thanks, Dad," she said.

"Can we do anything to help?" eighteen-year-old Nicholas Morrow asked sympathetically.

Mrs. Wakefield shook her blond head. "You and David have been heroes already," she told him. "Thank you, too, sergeant," she added, leaning across the desk to shake his hand.

"Come *on*!" Jessica wailed, tugging at her mother's hand. "We've got to go see what's happened to George and Enid!"

Nobody said a single word on the way to the hospital. And Elizabeth, for one, was grateful for the silence. She wasn't going to breathe easy until she saw her best friend with her own eyes and was convinced that Enid was really and truly all right.

"Mrs. Rollins?" Dr. MacGregor asked, stepping into the waiting room and looking at the attractive woman who was pacing outside his door. "Could you come into my office for a few minutes, please?"

Mrs. Rollins sank down on the chair closest to the doctor's desk. She had rushed to the Joshua Fowler Memorial Hospital the minute she got the phone call from the police. That had been almost two hours earlier, and she hadn't seen Enid or heard any news of her condition.

Mrs. Rollins had been divorced from her husband for some time. Enid was her only child, and now—watching the doctor take a file from his desk with her daughter's name on it—Mrs. Rollins couldn't help thinking that Enid was all she had in the world. If anything were seriously wrong . . .

"I'm afraid your daughter's situation is very grave," Dr. MacGregor said quietly, sitting down at his desk and opening the file. "Are you ready to hear this?" he asked Mrs. Rollins.

Enid's mother nodded. "Please," she said hoarsely. "Just tell me."

"She hit herself very hard at the base of the spine," Dr. MacGregor said slowly. "And I'm afraid the force of the blow was enough to damage the last disc in her spine. It's cutting off nerve communication to her legs."

"What does that mean, Dr. MacGregor?" Mrs. Rollins asked, her face draining of color.

"She's paralyzed," the doctor replied, looking down at his hands. "There's hope," he added quickly, taking a piece of paper out of the file. "We think an operation may relieve the pressure. But we won't know for a few days whether or not we can operate. We have to wait for the swelling to come down."

"My poor baby," Mrs. Rollins whispered, putting her face in her hands. "And George— Is George all right?" she demanded.

Dr. MacGregor sighed. "Yes," he told her. "He was incredibly lucky. It turns out the blow to his head wasn't as severe as we thought at first. His wound is mostly superficial. In fact, we've released him. But if it hadn't been for your daughter, Mrs. Rollins, he'd be dead. She saved his life."

Mrs. Rollins burst into tears. "Can I see her, doctor?"

Dr. MacGregor smiled gently. "I think it would be better if you went home and got some rest," he told her. "Enid is sound asleep. We've given her some drugs to reduce the pain, and she probably won't wake up until this evening. Why don't you come back then?"

"No," Mrs. Rollins said, smiling through her tears. "I'll just stay in the waiting room, then. And please let me know when I can see her."

*   *   *

George looked around furtively, making sure none of the nurses could see him. When the coast was clear, he sneaked into Enid's room, closing the door quietly behind him.

"You can go home now," the doctor had told him, fixing the bandage on his head with long strips of adhesive. But George couldn't go home without seeing Enid. He couldn't believe what the doctors had said when he'd asked about her condition. Paralyzed! His heart skipped a beat when he thought of that word.

On tiptoe he walked over to Enid's bed and stared down at her, his eyes filled with tears. She looked so innocent, he thought miserably, leaning over to brush a stray lock of hair from her face. She was sleeping soundly, a peaceful, almost serene expression on her lovely face.

"You saved my life," George whispered, taking her limp hand in his. "If it had't been for you, I'd be dead right now."

And if it hadn't been for me, you'd be perfectly fine, he added silently. *All this is my fault!* George felt sick with guilt when he remembered the doctor explaining to him exactly what Enid had done to hurt her spine—exactly what she'd gone through to save his life.

It was my fault, George thought miserably, blinking back tears. *All this was my fault*.

According to the emergency squad, there was no way to know what had made the plane's engine fail. They told George that the Federal

Aviation Administration would dredge the lake to find the plane. Only then would they be able to determine the reason for the crash.

But George was certain it was his inexperience that had caused the engine failure. Gripping Enid's hand tightly, he knelt by her side. "I'm going to make it up to you," he murmured. "I couldn't possibly tell you about Robin now—not after this. I'm going to keep it a secret. Because if *I* don't tell you, no one can. No one can hurt you by telling you the truth."

Except, he remembered with a pang, Elizabeth Wakefield. Enid's best friend already knew the truth. She had confronted Robin and George that morning at the airfield, and they'd told her how they felt.

But Elizabeth won't tell Enid, he thought desperately. *I won't let her! Enid mustn't find out what happened between Robin and me.*

Pushing his face against Enid's warm neck, George felt a sob rising in his chest. "How could I have done this to you?" he cried.

Enid didn't move. The drugs the doctors had given here were so powerful she couldn't feel George's arms around her. She was still sleeping peacefully when he crept out of the room, tears of guilt and sorrow streaking his handsome face.

It was after midnight, and Elizabeth Wakefield was wide awake. She still couldn't believe the events that had occurred that afternoon. At the

22

hospital Elizabeth and her family had had to wait well over an hour before they were even allowed up to the floor where Enid's room was located. When they arrived upstairs, Mrs. Rollins was talking to one of the doctors. But the Wakefields didn't have to wait long to learn what had happened to Enid.

"George is fine," Mrs. Rollins told Mr. Wakefield. "Just a few bad bumps and a cut on the side of his head. He's gone home already. But Enid—"

"Enid!" Elizabeth had gasped, clutching at Jessica for support.

"She's seriously hurt," Mrs. Rollins said gently, tears welling in her eyes. "Dr. MacGregor is hoping to operate in a few days, once the swelling at the base of her spine has gone down. But until then—"

"How bad is it?" Mr. Wakefield asked, putting his arm around Mrs. Rollins.

Mrs. Rollins sighed, a tear trickling down her cheek. "I'm afraid right now she's paralyzed," she said quietly. "And the doctor has no idea yet if the operation will restore the nerve communication to her legs. We'll just have to wait."

"We'll just have to wait," Elizabeth repeated bitterly to herself now, lying rigid in her bed, her eyes wide open. *"George is fine,"* she heard Mrs. Rollins saying for what must have been the fiftieth time this evening. *George is fine, but Enid—*

23

It's just wasn't fair! Elizabeth thought, turning over and pushing her face into the pillow. *It wasn't fair that George should just walk away with a few stitches, while Enid—*

But she couldn't even think about Enid lying paralyzed in her hospital bed. It was too terrible. And nothing her parents or Todd had said to console her had made her feel any better. They didn't know, she thought angrily. They didn't know what she knew about George Warren. He didn't even love Enid anymore, and she'd done this to herself so she could save his life!

The irony was too much for Elizabeth to bear. Enid was her dearest friend, one of the kindest, most giving people she had ever known. And George Warren—well, he'd been one of her closest friends until that morning.

But now . . .

Elizabeth couldn't even face how she felt about George right now. All she knew was that she had to help Enid somehow. She had to pray that the operation would help, and she had to pray, however much it sickened her, that George would forget Robin now and give Enid all the love and attention he had.

Because without that, Elizabeth knew, Enid might never recover at all.

Three

On Monday Jessica thought twice about going to the gourmet cooking class she'd signed up for after school. Elizabeth had planned to go to the hospital after her last-period class, and Jessica felt as though she ought to go with her—even if they couldn't see Enid—just to give her twin moral support.

Besides, Jessica wasn't very excited about starting the cooking class. It had been Lila Fowler's idea, and now that she and Lila weren't on speaking terms, it seemed like a waste of time.

But Elizabeth, surprisingly enough, had talked her twin into going. "It's the first class," she pointed out. "If you miss it, you'll never catch up. Besides, I called the hospital at lunch. They're not going to let Enid have visitors for another day or two."

But by the time Jessica was installed behind a small counter in the spotless room in the Sweet Valley Civic Center, where the class was held, she knew she'd made a mistake. The instructor wasn't even on time, and Ms. Jackson, the petite gray-haired lady who helped run the civic center, had to get the class started. The project for the first class was to make mustard, and each student had been given a mortar and pestle, and a bag of mustard seeds.

"Now remember, class," Ms. Jackson said cheerfully, "the recipe calls for *finely ground* mustard seeds. Just pound away with your pestles. Your instructor will be with you in a few minutes!"

I'll bet, Jessica said to herself, scowling. She poured mustard seeds into her mortar and began smashing them as hard as she could with the pestle. Three times a week! Jessica thought. How was she going to stand this class? She had been an idiot for listening to Lila go on and on about how important it was to know how to make elegant dishes. Elegant dishes! And what were they making today? Mustard!

Just in case Lila had missed the sulky scowl on her face, Jessica began to mutter aloud as she whacked the mustard seeds with the pestle. "Of all the stupid wastes of time," she seethed.

Lila, her pretty light-brown head bent studiously over her own work, didn't look up.

Jessica and Lila had had rough spots in their friendship before, but none so serious as the breach that had occurred recently over Jack. It was true that Lila had met Jack first, Jessica admitted. So maybe it really hadn't been fair for her to get involved with him. But Jack had sworn to her that he was through with Lila, that he cared only for Jessica. How was she supposed to know he'd been swearing the same thing to Lila?

A particularly violent whack of Jessica's pestle spurted a dollop of brownish gook on the sleeve of Lila's cream-colored silk blouse. "OK, Jess, that's it," Lila said furiously.

"What's it?" Jessica asked innocently.

"Do you realize," Lila pointed out, "that this blouse cost ninety dollars at Lisette's?"

Jessica shrugged. Everything Lila owned was ridiculously expensive. As the daughter of George Fowler, one of the richest men in town, Lila was used to getting what she wanted—and what she wanted tended to cost a bundle.

Jessica was in no mood to feel guilty. "This class is an utter waste," she hissed. "Who wants to waste time pounding mustard seeds? I thought we were going to learn to make something fun!"

Lila pouted. "I don't want to talk to you," she said. "Not about mustard or anything else. Not after what you did to me."

"You!" Jessica exclaimed. "*I'm* the one who had my life threatened. I think I did you a favor."

Lila didn't look convinced. "Jack never told me he was seeing you," she said petulantly. "It wasn't very nice of you, Jess."

Jessica considered for a moment. "I guess it wasn't," she admitted. Usually Jessica didn't think twice about stealing a boy from someone else, but she didn't want Lila to think she was so hard up for guys she had to get them second-hand. "I guess he deceived both of us, huh?" she ventured.

Lila's haughty face relaxed into a smile. Jessica was too good a friend to stay mad at for long, and besides—as Elizabeth had found out far too often—it was hard to stay angry with Jessica once she put on the charm.

"Truce?" Jessica said winningly.

Lila sighed. "Truce."

"Now, if I can just interrupt you chefs-in-training for a second," Ms. Jackson chimed in from the front of the room, "I'd like to introduce you to Jean-Pierre Baptiste, who will be your teacher. Monsieur Baptiste is the author of several cookbooks, and the youngest head chef ever at La Maison Blanche, one of the finest French restaurants in California."

"Good Lord," Jessica whispered, her pestle falling out of her hand and crashing to the floor. Without a doubt, Jean-Pierre was the handsomest man she'd ever seen, she thought breathlessly.

In his early twenties, Jean-Pierre was well over six feet tall, his broad shoulders tapering down to a slender waist. He had jet black hair worn a bit longer than that of most of the guys Jessica knew at school, and chiseled features that looked like those of one of the statues she'd seen in slides in her art class. And his eyes— Jessica had never seen such intense blue eyes before.

"Good afternoon, class," Pierre said pleasantly. His French accent was so thick the words sounded magical. "I am happy to be here," he continued, sitting on the edge of the desk at the front of the room and smiling crookedly at his students. "I hope I can help you with your cooking and teach you"—he paused, as if searching for the English word—"all I know," he added, shrugging charmingly.

"Who cares about teaching?" Jessica muttered, her mouth dry.

"Maybe now you won't think this class is such a waste after all," Lila teased her.

"Waste?" Jessica asked, her blue-green eyes wide with disbelief. She had fallen in love with a real European man—and quite simply the most gorgeous European man in the whole world. "Waste?" she repeated senselessly. "Lila Fowler, you're the best friend in the whole world!"

Jessica had never paid as close attention to anything as she did to Jean-Pierre's lesson in the next half hour. She mixed white wine and vinegar and a pinch of sugar and salt into the brownish-yellow powder her hammering had produced—all just as Jean-Pierre instructed—and the whole time all she could think about was falling madly in love with him and flying back to France with him, living in one of those wonderful châteaus, and kissing him under the Eiffel Tower.

But much as Jessica loved to daydream, she

was far too practical to think of Jean-Pierre only in terms of France.

The Eiffel Tower was one thing. But what Jessica really had on her mind was the dance coming up in a few weeks. Jessica had been racking her brains, trying to think of someone interesting to go with, and now this gorgeous creature had just fallen into her lap.

If it kills me, I've got to learn to do this right, Jessica told herself, stirring the unappetizing mixture before her as hard as she could. *Because if the way to Jean-Pierre's heart is through his stomach, I've got my work cut out for me!*

"You don't mind stopping by Robin Wilson's house on the way home, do you?" Jessica asked sweetly, hopping into the passenger seat of Lila's lime-green Triumph.

Lila wrinkled her nose. "What do you want with Robin?" she demanded.

"She is the co-captain of the cheerleading squad," Jessica pointed out, tucking her mason jar of mustard under her feet as she swung the car door closed. "And I've got to let her know we're changing cheerleading practice tonight. Come on, Lila. It's just a few blocks out of the way."

"All right," Lila grumbled, turning the key in the ignition. "Did Cara tell you that Robin broke up with Allen this weekend?" she added a moment later, backing the car out of the parking space.

"You're kidding," Jessica said, unwrapping a stick of gum. "What for? I thought they were crazy about each other?"

"Some other guy," Lila said with a shrug. "Cara only found out because she's Allen's lab partner in chemistry. But he wouldn't tell her who the guy was. Cara figures he doesn't know himself."

"Hmm," Jessica said thoughtfully. "You don't suppose—"

"Don't suppose what?" Lila demanded.

Jessica shook her head. "Never mind," she said. "Hey, slow down! You're going to go past it!" she warned. They had just come to Robin Wilson's house, and Jessica's eyes narrowed as she saw the light-blue GTO in the driveway. She'd know that car anywhere, Jessica thought uneasily. It was George Warren's.

And there was George, walking down Robin's front walk toward the driveway.

"Never mind, Lila," Jessica said. "I can tell Robin about cheerleading later. Let's get out of here."

"What's the matter, Jess?" Lila asked, surprised.

"Nothing," Jessica said shortly.

"You don't think George Warren is the reason Robin and Allen broke up, do you?" Lila pressed her.

Jessica bit her lip. "Did Cara tell you what

Robin did at Secca Lake yesterday? She passed out cold when the crew carried George to the ambulance on a stretcher."

As she drove Lila glanced quickly at Jessica. "It looks like a closed case, then, Jess. Why else would George be at Robin's right now?"

"Still," Jessica added indignantly, "you'd think he'd wait till Enid was out of the hospital to start cheating on her!"

Lila shrugged. Cheating was still a sore subject with her. "Don't let it bother you," she said. "You're going to have your hands full with Jean-Pierre. Remember?"

Jessica smiled, but her blue-green eyes were serious. She didn't like what she had just seen one bit. And she had a feeling that Elizabeth was going to like it a whole lot less.

George turned his GTO down a tree-lined side street in Sweet Valley, oblivious to the beauty of the sunlight streaming through the lush foliage. His mother had urged him to stay home that afternoon. "Dr. MacGregor said you need a lot of rest," she'd told him. But George couldn't sleep. The pills he'd taken the previous night had knocked him out for a few hours, but he'd slept fitfully, waking from terrible dreams with feelings of confusion and horror.

Now he was on his way back from Robin's house. He had hoped to find her at home, but no one had answered when he'd rung the bell. "It's probably just as well," George told himself. He knew what he had to tell Robin wasn't going to be easy. But he'd convinced himself that it was cowardly not to tell her in person, which was why he'd gone to her house.

But it probably would be easier on the telephone, he told himself now. Just thinking about Robin and her reaction to what he had to tell her made tears spring to his eyes. He had never meant for this to happen, but he was deeply in love with her. And the anguish he'd experienced since the accident the day before hadn't diminished his affection.

Still, he reminded himself, he owed Enid his life. And as long as she was in serious condition, he wasn't going to abandon her. Maybe when she was better—

But it seemed too unfair to Enid to hope that things would ever work out between Robin and him. No, he would just have to explain to Robin that they were through for good, he told himself firmly.

And that was exactly what he would have done that afternoon if she'd been home. Now he would have to resort to the phone. Because it just wasn't a good idea for people to see the two of them together, he decided.

He was thinking about Lila Fowler's green Triumph. He'd seen the car slow down as he walked down the Wilson's front walk. He hadn't been able to get a good look at the girl in the passenger seat, but he'd recognized Lila's car right away. And whoever was with her was facing his direction.

Ordinarily George couldn't have cared less about gossip. But he knew Enid would be terribly hurt if people started talking about Robin and him. And he had to do everything in his power to make sure Enid didn't get hurt any more. It was bad enough that she's paralyzed. If she thought he didn't love her on top of everything that had happened . . .

What worried George most was Elizabeth Wakefield. He knew how much she cared about Enid, and he couldn't imagine her deliberately hurting her best friend. But he also knew how much Elizabeth respected honesty. She would despise him for faking it with Enid, he thought miserably. And Elizabeth just might tell Enid why. If only he could take back all those things he had told Elizabeth! If she didn't know how much he and Robin loved each other, everything would be so much easier!

Well, he'd just have to convince her—and anyone else who suspected—that it was all over between Robin and him. As long as Enid was suffering, he owed her all the time and love he had.

George sighed as he pulled the GTO into his garage. He wondered if Robin would understand when he told her it was all over between them—for now, and for good.

*   *   *

"Wait a minute," Elizabeth said, sitting up on her bed and blinking at Jessica. "You saw George *where?*"

It was late afternoon, and Elizabeth was trying to take a quick nap, having just come back from the hospital. As she'd been warned, she didn't get to see Enid, but at least she had been able to keep Mrs. Rollins company in the waiting room and to hear reports about how Enid looked.

"In front of Robin's house just now," Jessica repeated, rummaging around in her bag as she plopped onto the bed next to her twin. "I hope we're having something for dinner tonight that goes with mustard," she said doubtfully, pulling the mason jar out of her bag and displaying that afternoon's project.

"I don't believe it," Elizabeth said, her blue-green eyes darkening. "You saw George in front of Robin Wilson's house this afternoon?"

"Liz, are you going deaf?" Jessica complained. "I *told* you. I was on my way back from my cooking class. Lila gave me a ride, and I asked her to stop by Robin's so I could tell her we changed cheerleading from Monday to—"

"Jessica!" Elizabeth moaned. "Just tell me about George!"

Jessica looked injured. "I was about to." She sniffed. "First I saw George's car in the driveway. Then I saw George himself, strolling down the front walk. I think something weird is going on."

"Hmmm," Elizabeth murmured, sinking back

on the bed. "It's kind of hard to believe," she said carefully, fighting for control as she watched her sister's face. Inwardly Elizabeth felt a flash of anger so strong she almost winced. *How dare he!* she thought furiously. *How dare he go over and see Robin while Enid's lying helpless in that hospital bed!*

Elizabeth had promised herself that she would give George a chance for Enid's sake. It was one thing when she first found out George and Robin were seeing each other. That was bad enough. A phantom photographer had been submitting pictures to *The Oracle*, the school newspaper for which Elizabeth was a columnist. One of the pictures had shown George and Robin in an embrace. At first Elizabeth could hardly believe her eyes. But the day before, when she had gone out to the airfield to watch George get his diploma from his flying class, she knew it was true. There was no denying the way George and Robin were acting around each other. They were clearly in love.

At first Elizabeth had been furious, but when she listened to the couple, she realized they had a genuine conflict. Their affection for each other was legitimate, and they both knew that Enid would have to be told.

But now that the accident had occurred, Elizabeth didn't see how George could break the news to Enid. It would kill Enid, absolutely kill her, if she found out that George was in love with someone else. Elizabeth would never have believed that George would be low enough to keep seeing Robin while Enid was in the hospital. It was horrible! It made her so angry it was all she could do to keep her self-control.

And she wouldn't have kept her anger bottled up inside her if it weren't for Enid. If George was still seeing Robin, he must be doing in on the sly, Elizabeth decided. That was bad enough as far as she was concerned. But if Enid found out—if people started gossiping about George and Robin—

"Maybe we should keep quiet about it, Jess," she said finally. "It would be terrible if Enid heard about it."

Jessica looked indignant. "I wasn't going to tell anyone!" she protested. "Only you. But I'll tell you something, Liz. I'm not sure I'll be able to even look Robin Wilson in the face."

Elizabeth sighed. "I know what you mean," she agreed reluctantly. "To tell you the truth, Jess, the whole thing makes me so angry I could just—"

"Spit?" Jessica volunteered helpfully.

Elizabeth shook her head and burst out laughing. "That wasn't exactly what I had in mind," she told her twin. "Come on," she added. "Let's go see what'll go with mustard for dinner. I don't suppose hot dogs count as gourmet?"

"I don't know," Jessica said, looking worried. "What's French for hot dogs?"

Elizabeth got up from her bed and followed her twin downstairs. Secretly she couldn't help agreeing with Jessica. She wasn't looking forward to seeing Robin at school the next day. It was going to be pretty hard to act as though nothing was wrong. Her best friend was lying helpless in the hospital, and from what Jessica had just told her, it looked as if all George cared about was having more free time to spend with Robin.

It wasn't going to be easy to look either George or Robin in the eye without blowing up, Elizabeth thought. Not easy at all.

Four

"So you really think Robin's been seeing George behind Enid's back?" Cara asked, pushing her tray aside so she could put her elbows on the cafeteria table.

Jessica shrugged. "It sure seems that way, doesn't it?"

"I think that's absolutely *foul*!" Cara exclaimed, wrinkling her nose in disgust. "Poor Enid," she added. "Do they have any more news about her condition?"

"It doesn't sound too good," Jessica said mournfully, taking the wrapper off a Popsicle. Jessica's sympathy for Enid Rollins was a recent development. Before the plane crash Jessica had had several conversations with her sister about her choice of friends, and Enid got most of the criticism. In Jessica's opinion Enid Rollins was just plain *boring*.

But the accident had changed Enid in Jessica's eyes. Now Sweet Valley High was buzzing with talk about Enid—everyone wondered how she was feeling, if there was any progress, any hope. It was all terribly exciting, and naturally Jessica, as the twin sister of Enid's very best friend, was right at the center of all the speculation.

Moreover, Jessica really did feel sorry for Enid. She had never thought much of George Warren one way or another, but now she was prepared to see him as a villain.

And Robin Wilson, whom Jessica had become rather fond of over the past few months, suddenly seemed like an evil temptress. Robin certainly had come far this year, Jessica had to admit. At the beginning of the year, she'd been plump and plain and a virtual nothing. When she'd tried to pledge Pi Beta Alpha, the popular sorority Jessica headed, Jessica had blackballed her.

A strict diet-and-exercise regime had helped Robin to become one of the prettiest girls in the junior class. Since Robin had been elected co-captain of the cheerleading squad, she and Jessica had been thrown together fairly often. And Jessica enjoyed her company.

But when Jessica went on a rampage, there was no stopping her. *Fair's fair*, she told herself. *Robin shouldn't see George behind Enid's back. And that's all there is to it.*

"So how do you think we should handle Robin?" Cara asked, looking outside to the patio, where Robin was finishing her lunch.

"Cold war," Jessica said grimly. "All out cold

war. And," she added slyly, fiddling with the wrapper from her Popsicle, "maybe it wouldn't be such a bad idea to let everyone else in on the plan. What do you think?"

"I think she deserves it!" Cara exclaimed, her dark eyes sparkling. "After all," she added, getting up from the table and pushing in her chair, "it's the least we can do for poor Enid."

"You're absolutely right," Jessica said solemnly, her eyes narrowing as she followed Cara's gaze to the patio outside.

"Wait a minute!" Cara said. "It looks like Robin's coming over here right now!"

"Just remember," Jessica reminded her, *"cold war."*

"Jess," Robin said, pulling out a chair and sitting at their table, "I've been looking for you everywhere. Why didn't you tell me cheerleading practice got changed? I waited outside the gym for half an hour last night."

Jessica didn't answer.

"Is something wrong?" Robin added, looking confused.

"Come on, Cara," Jessica said suddenly, jumping out of her chair. "I just remembered I've got to call the hospital and see how Enid's doing."

"Don't you think that was a little harsh?" Cara whispered as they hurried away, leaving Robin staring blankly after them.

"Not at all," she replied. "We have to do what we can to help Enid, don't we?"

41

"I guess so." Cara sighed and turned to look back at Robin. *Jessica's right,* she told herself, *and it's no use getting softhearted about the whole thing. Robin deserves everything she gets.*

But Cara had to admit that Robin looked awfully lonely and confused. And despite what Jessica had said, Cara couldn't help feeling a little sorry for her.

It's got to be my imagination, Robin Wilson thought uneasily. *Why in the world would Jessica and Cara be angry with me?* But the uneasy feeling still remained.

I'm just getting paranoid, Robin decided, looking hungrily at the ice cream Cara had left uneaten in her bowl. Robin couldn't help it—when she got lonely or upset, she ate. And right now she was lonely *and* upset. A few days before she had been happier than she'd ever been. And now she couldn't imagine how she was going to make it from one day to the next.

The day George's plane had crashed had been the worst in Robin's life. Her first reaction had been sheer terror. When she saw George being carried by the ambulance crew, his face covered with blood, she couldn't care less if anyone was watching. All she knew was that George was in trouble. And the next thing she knew she was flat on the ground and someone was wiping her forehead with a cold cloth.

When she came to, she realized she couldn't

let anyone know how upset she was. So she didn't try to call the hospital until she got home. By then, George had been released, the nurse had told her. And she'd been so relieved she'd almost burst into tears then and there. But Enid . . .

As soon as Robin learned that Enid was in serious condition, she knew that George couldn't leave her. It would be impossible. Even so, his phone call the night before had been incredibly painful.

"We can't see each other anymore, Robin," George had said quietly. "Not at all. Not unless—" And his voice had broken off, choked with emotion. "If we run into each other, we have to act like we're just casual friends," he added. And she knew he was right.

But the thought of never seeing George again was too painful to imagine. Robin wasn't sure which was more painful, her guilt over Enid or her sorrow over losing George. And to top it all off, she had to face Allen at school every day. He looked so miserable.

Robin looked up and saw Elizabeth and Todd walking by. "Liz!" she called quickly.

Elizabeth turned, her pretty face expressionless.

"Have you heard anything about Enid?" Robin asked.

Elizabeth sighed. "She's still about the same," she said quietly. "I'll let you know if I hear there's a change," she added, taking Todd's hand and walking away.

Tears of pain stung Robin's eyes. *Was Elizabeth mad at her, too?* she wondered. *That was more than she could take.*

Afraid that she was going to burst into tears any second, Robin took a deep breath, got up from her table, and headed back through the cafeteria to the food counter. "A piece of chocolate cake," she mumbled to the woman near the desserts. "Oh, and put some ice cream on top," she added miserably, digging in her pockets for some money.

It wouldn't matter if she did get fat again, she thought glumly, taking her dessert back to the table. It didn't look as though she had any friends left to notice.

"Liz!" Enid cried softly, reaching out to her best friend. "I'm so glad you've come," she added, her eyes filling with tears.

Elizabeth sat down on a chair next to Enid's hospital bed. "I came the minute they'd let me!" She laughed. "I've been driving the nurses crazy for the last few days!"

Enid smiled. "I know," she said. "They finally let George come today, too. He's just down the hall now, getting a drink of water," she added.

Elizabeth didn't say anything. "How are you, Enid?" she asked seriously, squeezing her friend's hand tightly.

Enid lowered her eyes. When she looked up again, her face was perfectly composed. "It's not that bad, Liz," she said gently. "Oh, I admit it's scary. I still can't get used to not being able to feel anything in my legs. But the doctors think they may be able to operate in a few days. And the important thing—"

"What's the important thing?" George asked, walking into the room with a paper cup of water. "Hi, Liz," he said after a moment, looking at her with a mixutre of pain and embarrassment.

Liz nodded but said nothing.

Enid said softly, "I was just going to say that what really matters is we're both alive."

George blushed. "She's amazing," he said to Elizabeth. "Do you realize she saved my life?"

Elizabeth looked at him gravely. "I know."

Enid looked from Elizabeth to George, her brow wrinkling. "Don't be so serious, you two. All I get around here are doctors and nurses. Why don't you tell me all the gossip?"

George's blush deepened. "There isn't any," he said hastily, not looking at Elizabeth.

"Jessica's taking a gourmet cooking class," Elizabeth said and giggled. "In fact, she made a present for you. I'm not sure how it tastes," she added, taking out the box Jessica had packed that afternoon, "but it sure sounds fancy. It's a raspberry torte."

Enid burst out laughing, her green eyes lighting up. "What's Jessica doing in a cooking class?" she asked.

Elizabeth smiled. It was so good to see Enid looking cheerful. "I think it may have something to do with Jean-Pierre, the chef who's teaching the class," she confided. "You know Jess. There's a big dance coming up, and I think she's decided to look for a date from outside school."

"It looks awfully good," Enid said, opening the box. "Not like Jess." She giggled. "Are you sure Jessica made it herself?" she asked doubtfully. "This guy must be fabulous to warrant this kind of effort!"

George hadn't said a word. Uncomfortable, he was standing near the foot of Enid's bed, listening to the conversation and smiling awkwardly.

"I'd forgotten all about the dance," Enid added. For just a minute a wistful expression came over her face, and Elizabeth thought how hard it must be for her, lying in a hospital bed unable to move while life at school went on as normal.

"George, don't you want to sit down?" Enid asked, turning her head to give him a warm smile.

George looked nervously down at his feet. "I think I'd better be going soon," he told her, still avoiding Elizabeth's gaze. "I'm staying home from school this week, and I promised my mother I'd pick up some things at the store for dinner."

"Oh," Enid said, looking crestfallen. "OK. Can you come back tomorrow?" she asked eagerly.

"Of course I can," George murmured, leaning over the bed and kissing her softly. "Take care of yourself," he added quickly, giving her blanket an awkward pat. " 'Bye, Liz," he said almost as an afterthought when he'd reached the door.

Enid was quiet for a minute after George had gone. "I'm so worried about him," she told Elizabeth. "Sometimes I think . . . well, what if I'd lost him? It would've been so terrible."

Elizabeth swallowed the lump that was rising in her throat. Poor Enid! She looked so helpless. Her ivory complexion was even paler than usual, framed by her soft brown hair. It upset Elizabeth to see Enid so trusting, so innocent. Here she was worrying about losing George—and Elizabeth knew she'd already lost him.

"Enid," she murmured, giving her friend's hand another squeeze, "don't worry about a thing. You just rest and get well. OK?"

"OK," Enid whispered. "Come back soon," she added. "Liz, seeing you two is the best thing that's happened in days!"

"I'll be back tomorrow," Elizabeth promised. "And be sure to let me know if there's anything I can bring you."

"I'll let you know," Enid said, trying hard to smile.

As Elizabeth closed the door to Enid's room, she sighed. She knew what Enid needed more than anything in the world was George's love. She had sacrificed herself so unthinkingly for

47

him, and now she needed to know that he loved her.

And that, Elizabeth thought sadly, *is something I can't bring Enid, no matter how hard I try.*

"The Federal Aviation Administration called while you were at the hospital," Mrs. Warren told George as he sank into one of the chairs at the kitchen table. "They wanted to let you know that they found the plane this morning. They're going to take the engine apart to see if they can find out why it stalled."

"Thanks, Mom," George said quietly. He was certain that they wouldn't find anything wrong with the engine. It was his inexperience that had caused the crash. He knew he'd panicked too much to be able to control the plane once the engine cut out. Even if the board didn't take his license away, he knew he'd never fly again. Not after this.

Seeing Enid had been much harder than he'd expected. Try as he would, he couldn't act natural with her. He felt as if he had guilt written all over his face. She looked so helpless, lying in that bed, and every time he looked at her he felt like crying.

And when Elizabeth arrived, he thought, it was just unbearable. He had a feeling Elizabeth wouldn't tell Enid about their conversation at the airfield—not for his sake, but for Enid's. Even so, she knew. And the grave expression in her blue-green eyes had almost driven him mad.

I don't know if I'm going to be able to go through with this, George thought weakly, rubbing the bandage on his head. *Just being with Enid makes me feel so cheap, so dishonest.*

But he had no alternative, he reminded himself. He had to pull himself together and act as though nothing was wrong. He just had to!

Stifling a sob, George headed upstairs to his room. For the time being, all he wanted was to be alone.

Five

Elizabeth and George were sitting stiffly in the waiting room on the sixth floor of the Joshua Fowler Memorial Hospital, waiting to see Enid. The night before, after Elizabeth had gotten home, she'd received a telephone call from Mrs. Rollins. Dr. MacGregor had decided it was time to operate. The swelling had subsided sufficiently, and now they'd be able to look at the disc that was cutting off the nerve communication to Enid's legs.

"I know she'll want to see you before the operation," Mrs. Rollins had told Elizabeth. "She's being so brave, Liz, but I think she's scared to death."

"Of course I'll be there," Elizabeth had told her, even though she knew she'd have to miss some of her afternoon classes to go to the hospital.

Mrs. Rollins was with Enid now.

"God, it's terrible waiting!" George burst out, staring helplessly at Elizabeth.

Elizabeth picked a magazine up from the chair next to her and opened it. "Just imagine how Enid must feel," she remarked. *And quit feeling sorry for yourself*, she added silently.

"Liz," George said, "we have to talk. If you only knew—"

"What could we possibly have to talk about?" Elizabeth interrupted, keeping an eye on the door to the waiting room. She didn't want Mrs. Rollins to find her quarreling with George. But she was too fed up with him to keep quiet a minute longer.

"Liz, it's all over between Robin and me!" George insisted, running his hands through his hair. "I swear it is! After what happened—"

Elizabeth stared at him. *Is that why you went over to see Robin the other day?* she wondered. She was convinced George wasn't telling the truth. And when she thought of Enid, waiting to be wheeled to the operating room . . .

"George? Liz?" Mrs. Rollins said, stepping into the waiting room. "You can go in and see her now," she told them, trying to smile.

Elizabeth let George go into Enid's room ahead of her. She wanted to compose her face before she saw her friend, afraid some of the anger would show in her eyes. But she needn't have worried. The minute she saw Enid her anger melted.

"How are you?" she asked her friend anxiously, dropping into the chair next to her bed. Elizabeth's breath caught in her throat when she looked at Enid. She'd never seen her friend so pale—and there were tears shining in Enid's eyes.

"I'm scared," Enid whispered, looking from Elizabeth to George. "I'm so scared."

George cleared his throat nervously. "Don't be," he told her, taking her hand and giving it a squeeze. "Dr. MacGregor knows exactly what he's doing. And from what he's said, I have a feeling you'll be walking out of here in no time at all."

Elizabeth bit her lip and stared at the linoleum tiles covering the hospital floor. She wished she could feel as optimistic as George. But all she could think of over and over again, was the terrifying thought: *What if the operation doesn't work?*

She couldn't let Enid see how worried she was. "George is right," she said firmly. "Dr. MacGregor is the best there is. You're going to be just fine, Enid."

Enid shook her head, tears rolling down her pale cheeks. "I don't know what I'd do without you guys," she whispered. "I feel like I've got to be brave, for your sake. Liz, I keep thinking about when you and Todd got in that motorcycle accident and everyone was afraid—" She stopped talking, her voice choked with tears.

Elizabeth shuddered. That accident was one of the worst things that had ever happened to her, and each time she set foot in this hospital she remembered it. "And look how well I turned out!" she said as cheerfully as she could.

"And, George," Enid said softly, stroking his hand. "You're always so brave. If it weren't for you . . ." She turned her head aside, tears spilling onto the pillow. "I don't know what I'd do if it weren't for you," she sobbed. "I don't think I could go on."

George looked quickly at Elizabeth before leaning over the bed. "You don't have to worry about that," he said firmly. "I'm not going anywhere. I'll be right here at your side as long as they'll let me."

Enid's eyes widened as if she'd just remembered the ordeal she was about to face. "Will you both be outside the whole time?" she demanded. "Will you be in the waiting room the whole time I'm in the operating room?"

George nodded gravely. "I promise," he whispered, leaning over to kiss her cheek.

Elizabeth sighed. She didn't feel quite so angry with George anymore. He was suffering, too. She only wished he were still in love with Enid.

But she wasn't about to let Enid see the wistful expression in her eyes. "I'll be right outside, too," she whispered, giving her friend a hug. "I know you're going to be just fine, Enid. I can feel it."

"Thank you," Enid murmured sadly, lying back on the pillow. "Thank you both."

Just then a pretty young nurse came into the room with a clipboard in her hand. "Sorry, you two," she said brightly, "but I'm going to have to ask you to leave now. We've got to get Enid ready."

Elizabeth felt a terrible uneasiness in her stomach as she followed George out into the waiting room. Her last glance at Enid didn't do much to console her. She looked so small and frail in that huge bed.

Thank heavens Mrs. Rollins would be at the hospital with George and her, she thought gratefully. The long hours of waiting for the results of the operation would be unbearable if she and George were left alone.

Even as it was, she thought unhappily, she had a feeling this would be one of the longest afternoons of her life!

It was three o'clock, and Jessica was unwrapping the pastry she'd put in the refrigerator after the last class. "Today we are making *pâte feuilletée*, puff pastry," Jean-Pierre announced, and Jessica's heart beat louder the second she heard his voice. "This is one of the greatest challenges a chef can face," he added, his accent making the ordinary words sound so sexy Jessica couldn't believe it. "We must try very hard to insure the pastry is light and flaky."

"Who's he kidding," Lila grumbled, poking at her dough with the tips of her fingers. "This stuff feels slimy," she whispered to Jessica. "I think you were right, Jess. This class is a waste of time."

"Waste?" Jessica echoed indignantly, sprinkling flour on her pastry marble so the dough wouldn't stick. "It's not a waste! I think it's terribly important to know how to cook."

Lila snorted. "I don't suppose Jean-Pierre has anything to do with your new obsession?" she asked slyly.

Jessica smiled dreamily, kneading the dough with both hands. "Just imagine," she crooned. "Jean-Pierre will take me back to Paris with him and let me cook in one of his restaurants. People from all over the world will rave about my light, flaky pastry. And Jean-Pierre will be so impressed he won't be able to stop himself. He'll fall madly in love with me. And—"

"You're crazy, Jess," Lila grumbled, sprinkling flour on her marble gingerly so she wouldn't get her blouse covered with it. "I think you've really gone off the deep end this time. He's way too old for you, for one thing. And for another—"

"It's different in European countries, Lila," Jessica said dismissively, dotting her dough with butter. "I can guarantee you, Jean-Pierre and I are meant for each other. Did you see what a big deal he made out of my mustard?"

Lila shook her head. "I mean it, Jess," she continued. "This time you've really completely flipped."

"Just between you and me," Jessica added, folding her dough over, "I have a feeling Jean-Pierre's going to be my date for the dance the

55

week after next. I can just sort of sense that things are about to happen."

"The only thing that's about to happen is that little men in white coats are going to come drag you away," Lila muttered.

"Now *this*," Jean-Pierre exclaimed, stopping beside Jessica as he made his way around the room, "is exactly the way the dough should look before rolling."

To Jessica's delight, he picked her dough up to display it to the other students. "You are a natural," he told her, smiling. "I expect even better things from you in the future."

"You see?" Jessica whispered when Jean-Pierre had moved away. "What did I tell you?"

Lila looked down at the grayish ball she had formed and sniffed. "You can *have* Jean-Pierre and all this stupid glop," she told her. "I'm getting fed up with the whole thing."

Jessica grinned as she rolled her dough out flat. *She* wasn't sick of the class—not at all. And Jean-Pierre wasn't the only reason why she was still interested.

Jessica Wakefield had come up with a brilliant idea.

For as long as Jessica could remember, Elizabeth had always outshone her when it came to giving gifts. It wasn't that Jessica didn't have good ideas. It was just that Elizabeth was so hard to compete with! Liz was perfect at everything, Jessica thought, sighing, and she was organized, thoughtful, loving. She never forgot an important date or failed to come up with a meaningful gift just at the right time or place.

The Wakefields' wedding anniversary was the date Jessica had always had the hardest time remembering. And Elizabeth always made her feel like a jerk, giving their parents a present when Jessica had forgotten all about it. *But this year I haven't forgotten*, she thought with a triumphant smile. *And Liz isn't going to show me up this time!*

Before she'd started the class, Jessica hadn't been enthusiastic about the idea of learning to cook. But Jean-Pierre's enthusiasm was beginning to effect her. She felt tremendously encouraged, and she was sure now she could make a really special, romantic dinner for her parents— one they'd never forget.

Maybe she could even ask Jean-Pierre for help, she thought with a sly smile. He could advise her on the menu—and, one thing might lead to another, and they might end up planning on going to the dance together after all. Stranger things had happened!

Jessica couldn't help humming as she cut her dough. There was nothing she loved as much as a good plan, and this scheme was particularly enjoyable. *I'm through with being second best*, Jessica told herself, giving the dough a loving pat. *This time I'm going to make Mom and Dad proud of me!*

And if she happened to win Jean-Pierre over while she was doing it, so much the better, she thought. She'd just consider it a bonus for work well done!

"Mrs. Rollins?" Dr. MacGregor said, stepping into the waiting room and taking off his surgical mask.

Enid's mother jumped to her feet, her face strained with anxiety. "How is she, doctor?" she managed.

Dr. MacGregor smiled, wiping his brow with one hand. "Your daughter's going to be just fine," he told her. "It was a tricky operation, and it took a lot longer than we expected, but I don't see any reason why she won't be able to resume normal activity within a short period."

"Thank God." George sighed and slumped back in his chair. His face had drained of color, and Elizabeth could see how relieved he was.

"Oh, Mrs. Rollins," Elizabeth gasped, jumping out of her chair and throwing her arms around Enid's mother, "I'm so happy for her!"

Mrs. Rollins hugged Elizabeth, then turned to the doctor.

"Can I see her?" she asked tearfully.

"Just for a minute or two," Dr. MacGregor said, smiling. "But what I wanted to tell you is that she's going to be very weak at first. Don't expect her to jump right out of bed and dance. She's shaken up by the whole thing, and it may take her awhile to get her old legs back. But we've set up physical therapy for her here in the hospital, and after she leaves she should come back as an outpatient every day until she has completely regained the use of her leg muscles."

"When can she come home?" Mrs. Rollins asked.

"Well, we'll have to see how she does. But I'm sure she'll be eager to get out of here, and if there are no complications, I don't see any reason why she can't go home next week."

"Family only," the doctor added as George and Elizabeth tried to follow Mrs. Rollins down the corridor toward Enid's room. "She's not conscious yet," he added gently. "But I'm sure she'll be delighted to see you both tomorrow."

Elizabeth bit her lip. This was the moment she'd been dreading. She was alone now with George, and the relief of learning that Enid was going to be all right had drained her so much she was afraid she might tell him what she really thought.

"Thank God," George said for the second time. "Whew," he added, wiping his forehead with the sleeve of his shirt. "I wouldn't want to live through another afternoon like this one for anything."

"I'm glad she's all right," Elizabeth said quietly.

"Look, Liz," George began. "We can't go on this way. I know you're upset with me about what happened with Robin, but I told you—all of that's finished. I wouldn't hurt Enid now for anything. Can't you believe that?"

Elizabeth traced the outline of the square of linoleum with the toe of her sandal. She wished she could believe it. But if it was true, why had George gone to see Robin the other day? And if he'd been hiding this from Enid for so long, how could Elizabeth possibly trust him now? "No," she said finally, turning away, "I can't."

"You have to!" George pleaded. "Don't you see," he pointed out, "how hard it would be on Enid if she thought things weren't perfect? After everything she's been through—"

Elizabeth spun on George, her eyes blazing with anger. "I don't think I need you to tell me how to treat my best friend. I'd never say a word to her about you and Robin. That's your business. But that doesn't mean I have to pretend that everything's fine when I'm talking to *you*, does it? When I think about how much Enid loves you, how trusting she is—and how she almost killed herself trying to save you—"

Elizabeth couldn't help herself. Tears were streaming down her face.

"Stop it!" George cried. "Liz, don't you think I've thought about all that? And Enid isn't the only one I've hurt," he added bitterly. "I hurt Robin, too. And because of me Robin hurt Allen. Don't you think I realize what I've done?"

Elizabeth shuddered. She didn't want to sympathize with George. It didn't seem fair. Enid was too close to her for that, and every time she recalled the way her best friend had looked before the operation she wanted to cry. But at the same time she couldn't help feeling for George. He looked so tired, so unhappy—

Elizabeth never got to finish her thought. Just then the door to the waiting room opened, and Mrs. Rollins came back in, her eyes shining with tears.

"She's OK," she whispered, shaking her head in disbelief. "The doctors say my baby's really OK. And they say she's going to walk again!"

"Of course she will," Elizabeth said soothingly, putting her arm around the exhausted woman. "She's going to be just fine."

"She looks so peaceful," Mrs. Rollins went on, dabbing at her eyes with a handkerchief. "Oh, I'm so relieved that she's going to be all right."

Elizabeth shot George a look as she helped Mrs. Rollins to the elevator. *We're all relieved*, she was thinking to herself. *I'm so happy for Enid that I could cry myself.*

One thing was keeping Elizabeth from sharing in Mrs. Rollins's joy. What was George going to do now that Enid's paralysis had been cured? Wouldn't this free him to do as he chose?

And there was no way of knowing how Enid— weak and vulnerable as she would be in the days following the operation—would take it when George made his true feelings known at last.

Six

Midafternoon sunlight streamed through the large windows in the student lounge, where Robin Wilson was reading the newspaper. It was her study hall, and she had lots of work she knew she ought to be doing. But she just couldn't keep her mind on anything lately. She'd turned two papers in late, and Ms. Taylor had shaken her head at Robin when she handed back the math test.

I'm making a mess of everything, Robin thought unhappily. To top it all off, she was beginning to gain weight. The only thing she'd been able to find in her closet that fit her that morning was an old wraparound shirt, left over from her "fat" days. *No more food for a while*, Robin had promised herself when she stepped off the scale. She'd gained ten pounds, and she hated the way she looked. *It took too long to get myself thin. I'm not going to let my figure go because my whole life is falling apart.*

But the boiled egg she'd had for breakfast and the small salad at lunchtime hadn't done much to cheer Robin up. And the more she thought about it, the more she had to feel gloomy about. In the first week following the plane crash, Robin had focused her attention on Enid's condition. The crash had occurred ten days ago. Now the news was all over school that Enid had gone home from the hospital and her doctor thought she'd be walking in days. Robin's first reaction had been tremendous relief, both for Enid and for George. Despite all that had happened, she still loved George, and she'd been suffering for him as long as Enid was in danger.

I'm so glad for Enid, she thought now, putting the newspaper aside and staring listlessly out the window. But Robin had to admit that her relief was mingled with misery. Not that she wasn't delighted Enid was going to be OK—that wasn't it at all.

The truth was that Robin had been unbearably lonely since the accident. Before she had met George in her flying class, she'd spent most of her time with Allen. After George, of course, seeing Allen was unfair. She could never have led him on, and she knew she had done the right thing when she'd told him they'd have to break up.

Now she didn't have Allen *or* George. George had stuck fast to his decision not to call her or drop by to see her, and she knew he was doing the right thing. It wouldn't be fair to hope he would change his mind, either. He owed it to Enid to stick by her as long as she needed him.

But Robin missed George terribly. She had never fallen in love this way before, and she had a feeling it was going to be a long, long time before she forgot him. No matter how often she reminded herself that George had to stand by Enid now, she found herself longing to see him—to hold him in her arms. Robin was also desperately in need of the companionship and advice of her close girlfriends now. They could have helped her to get through this rocky time.

But that was the hardest thing of all. For some reason that she didn't understand, Robin found that everyone she knew at school was avoiding her. At first she thought she was inventing the whole thing. But by now it was too obvious to ignore. Cara refused to sit next to her in history; DeeDee and Susan switched teams in gym class when Robin joined their group; Lila walked away from her when Robin tried to ask her a question; and Jessica changed two more cheerleading practices without telling her. *It's some kind of weird conspiracy*, Robin thought unhappily, *and I don't know why it's happening. All I know is that I want to stop it.*

The door opened, and Elizabeth Wakefield came in, a book in her hand. She spotted Robin and looked at her with dismay. She made a move as if to leave, but Robin jumped out of her chair and rushed over to her.

"Please don't go, Liz," she whispered. There

were other students in the room, and she didn't want them to overhear her. "I feel like I've got the plague or something!"

"What do you mean?" Elizabeth asked, closing the door behind her.

"Everyone's been avoiding me lately," Robin said miserably. "I've got no idea what I've done wrong. Please don't go."

Elizabeth sighed. "All right," she conceded, sinking into a chair across from Robin's.

Robin stared at her as she opened her book and began to leaf through the pages. *It's happening again*, she thought miserably, *She's going to avoid me too. I can't stand it any longer! She's just going to read her book and pretend I don't even exist!*

"Liz," she said impulsively, leaning forward in her chair, "what are you doing today after school?"

"Todd and I have plans," Elizabeth said. "Why?"

"I've got to talk to you," Robin said. "Do you think you could squeeze in a sundae with me at Casey's?"

Elizabeth shook her head, her blue-green eyes sympathetic. "Sorry," she said. "I promised Todd."

Robin's eyes filled with tears. "Liz, I'm begging you," she said desperately. "Something's going on around here, and I've got to talk to someone about it—someone I can trust. You're my only hope!"

Elizabeth sighed and lowered her book.

"OK," she said at last. "I'll meet you at Casey's at four o'clock."

She doesn't want to be seen with me! Robin thought miserably. *She's probably afraid if we walk over there together people will talk.*

For the life of her, Robin couldn't understand why Elizabeth—and everyone else she knew—was acting so strange around her. All she knew was that she had to do something about it soon.

Because if things go on this way much longer, Robin thought miserably, *I'm going to die of loneliness.*

The usual after-school hubbub filled Casey's when Elizabeth strolled back to a corner booth at five minutes to four. She wasn't surprised to see Robin waiting there for her already. The girl had sounded so urgent that Elizabeth had a feeling she'd been waiting quite a while. *She was probably afraid I wouldn't show up,* Elizabeth thought. The truth of the matter was she had thought about not coming. But it just seemed too unfair.

Elizabeth felt like a traitor as she slid into the booth across from Robin. Todd, as always, had been understanding about the change of plans. They were going to drop by Enid's house and see how she was doing. *I could hardly tell Enid I couldn't make it because I was meeting Robin Wilson to talk about George,* Elizabeth thought with a sigh. The more she thought about it, the less she understood why she had agreed to see Robin.

"What'll it be today, girls?" the waitress asked, taking out her note pad. Robin thought for a minute. "A hot fudge sundae," she said finally.

"Just an iced tea for me, please," Elizabeth said, and the waitress walked away.

Robin flushed. "I shouldn't have a sundae, really. I've started to put some weight back on."

"You look fine to me," Elizabeth fibbed. As a matter of fact, Robin *did* look as if she'd gained some weight. But Elizabeth hadn't come there to make small talk.

"Liz," Robin began nervously, fiddling with her napkin, "can I ask you womething?"

"Sure," Elizabeth replied. "What is it?"

"Is it my imagination, or have people been avoiding me lately?"

Elizabeth looked confused. "I'm not sure what you mean, Robin. Who's been avoiding you?"

"Well, what about you, for example?" Robin continued. "Haven't *you* been avoiding me?"

"Well," Elizabeth said after a moment. "I suppose in a way I have been."

"Why?" Robin demanded. "What have I done?"

Elizabeth leaned back in the booth and gripped the table with both hands. "I don't really feel comfortable talking about this," she said finally. "Robin, I think I'd better go."

"No, Liz, wait!" Robin cried. "Please tell me!" she begged. "I really want to know what's going on!"

"Well," Elizabeth said finally, looking Robin straight in the eyes, "I didn't mean to avoid you, Robin, or hurt your feelings. But after what you and George told me that morning at the airfield, I feel kind of awkward around you. As long as Enid's still in such bad shape—"

Robin fiddled with her spoon. "But George and I are all through, Liz. Doesn't that change the way you feel?"

Elizabeth felt her face flushing. *Then why was George over at your house last Monday?* she wondered. Aloud all she could say was that she couldn't help her feelings—and she still felt awkward around both Robin and George.

"Well, just think how *I* feel, Liz," Robin complained. "No one at school will talk to me. And as for George—I've only spoken to him once since the accident. And that was to confirm what we both had decided independently—not to see each other again, unless—"

"Unless what?" Elizabeth demanded, her eyes flashing. "Unless Enid gets better, right?"

Robin stared dully at the tabletop. "George never said that," she admitted. "But I suppose if I'm honest, yes, I hope that happens! If Enid were to get completely better, why couldn't George tell her the way he'd planned to at first? The way I told Allen?"

Elizabeth jumped to her feet, her heart pounding. "I'm sorry, Robin, but I just can't listen to this. Enid is my best friend, and I can't bear to think—I mean Enid *isn't* all better! She's had a terrible shock. And if George were to break up with her—"

"George *won't* break up with her!" Robin cried. "Liz, you're not listening to me!"

"I can't listen," Elizabeth said unhappily. "I just can't be objective about this. I'm sorry, Robin, but I can't stand this any longer. I've got to go meet Todd."

Elizabeth hurried out of Casey's, her blond hair flying. She was too upset to look back at the corner booth she'd deserted. She'd had it with Robin and George, both of them. All she wanted now was for Enid to get better. That was the only thing that mattered.

"Is your friend coming back?" the waitress asked as she set down the sundae and the iced tea.

Robin shook her head, her eyes brimming with tears, "No," she mumbled, "she isn't."

None of them are, she told herself miserably. Sighing deeply, Robin began to eat the sundae.

"When do *I* get to cook dinner?" Jessica complained, looking critically at the barbecued chicken Mrs. Wakefield was bringing to the table.

"I don't know," Mrs. Wakefield said vaguely. "Are you sure you're really up to it, dear?"

"How's Enid?" Mr. Wakefield asked Elizabeth, taking a hot roll from the basket she passed him.

"Much better, according to Dr. MacGregor," Elizabeth told him. "But—"

"But what?" Mrs. Wakefield asked.

"I don't know," Elizabeth said slowly. "She hasn't been out of her wheelchair yet, and the doctor seemed to think she'd be able to walk right away."

"These things take longer than a week or two," Mrs. Wakefield said soothingly. "Don't worry about it, Liz. I'm sure in the next few days she'll—"

"Speaking of worry," Jessica interrupted, her mouth full of roll, "did Liz tell you we got a letter today about our jobs?"

"What jobs?" Mrs. Wakefield asked. "And don't interrupt, Jess. It's rude."

"Our tour-guide jobs," Jessica said. "We both got letters about it today. They're looking forward to having us work for them this summer, but there's one little catch."

"And what," Mr. Wakefield asked, sighing, "might that be?"

"Transportation," Jessica said mournfully. "They don't provide any to the tour center. And we'd have to take two buses to get there, which would take about an hour each way."

Since the fall, the twins had been looking forward to being tour guides along the scenic coastline near Sweet Valley. It was apparent from their faces that this snag was a real blow to them both.

"Can you believe it?" Jessica grumbled. "And

after we worked so hard at getting accepted. What are we going to do?"

"We might arrange a solution," Mr. Wakefield said, his eyes twinkling. "Don't you think so, Alice?"

"You mean one of you would be willing to drive us?" Jessica asked.

"Let's put them out of their misery." Mrs. Wakefield laughed. "Ned, isn't this a good time to tell the girls about the car?"

"What car?" Jessica demanded. "Are you guys breaking down and buying us a Jaguar?"

Mr. Wakefield burst out laughing. "Not quite," he told her. "But your mother and I have decided it's time that she got herself a new car. She could really use something a little newer, and, because of her interior design business, something a little bigger. And that means—"

"That Liz and I get the Fiat!" Jessica shrieked. "Ye!"

"As long as you're careful with it," Mrs. Wakefield warned. "And as long as you two manage to share it without killing each other. Is that a deal?"

"It's a deal," Elizabeth and Jessica said in unison, exchanging grins.

"Getting back to Enid," Elizabeth said thoughtfully. "Any objections to my having a small dinner party here on Friday evening? It'll just be Todd and me and George and Enid," she added hastily. "And I'll clean everything up. I

71

just wanted to have a kind of celebration for her. She may be walking by then!"

"It's fine with me," Mrs. Wakefield said. "We're going out on Firday night. Aren't we, Ned?"

"You're not kidding." Mr. Wakefield grinned. "We've got a date."

"What about you, Jess?" Elizabeth asked. "Have you got a date Friday night?"

Jessica pouted. "Not exactly," she said demurely. Her parents exchanged puzzled glances, and she sat up straighter in her chair, tossing her sun-streaked hair. "I mean, I *could* have a date if I wanted one," she explained. "But guys our age suddenly seem so *babyish* to me. Actually, I was planning on getting some cookbooks out of the library to read over the weekend. We're graduating to chicken cordon bleu next week, and I want to be ready."

"Is this the girl who turns up her nose at helping me barbecue hamburgers?" Mr. Wakefield asked.

"Hamburgers are gauche," Jessica told him. "What I like is called haute cuisine. You guys probably don't know what that means."

"Jessica," Mrs. Wakefield said warningly. "I hope your haute cuisine includes putting les dishes into la dishwasher."

"Not really," Jessica admitted, crestfallen. "Oh, all right," she grumbled, pushing her chair back. Taken as she was with cooking these days, Jessica still despised dishes.

"Do you want some help?" Elizabeth asked, hanging over the counter in the Spanish-tiled kitchen to watch Jessica at work.

"Well, as a matter of fact—" Jessica began sweetly.

"Good," Elizabeth said, too absorbed in her own thoughts to listen to her twin's response. "Then I think I'll go up and make a phone call." She walked away, leaving her twin staring after her.

As she dialed Todd's number, Elizabeth curled up in her favorite position in the armchair in her bedroom. But not even the prospect of hearing Todd's voice lifted her spirits.

She wasn't so sure her parents were right. Dr. MacGregor *had* said Enid should be on her feet by now.

And the way things were going, it didn't look as if Enid ever planned to get out of that wheelchair. Elizabeth had a terrible feeling that something was bothering Enid. Really bothering her.

And Elizabeth planned to find out what was going on the very first chance she got.

Seven

"This looks wonderful, Liz," Enid said appreciatively as Elizabeth carried a steaming bowl of spaghetti to the dining room table.

Elizabeth tried to smile. She had done everything she could to insure the night would be a success. She'd dimmed the lights in the Wakefield dining room, setting candles on the table to make the room look festive. And she'd used one of her mother's tried-and-true recipes for the spaghetti sauce. Todd had put some classical music on in the living room, and the total effect was charming.

Everything had seemed perfect until Enid and George arrived. "I can't believe it," Elizabeth whispered to Todd, watching George open the back door of his car and take out the folding wheelchair. "I was sure she'd be on her feet by now!" Once the wheelchair was reassembled, George opened the front door of the car and carefully lifted Enid in his arms.

"I can't bear it," Elizabeth said. "I can't stand the thought of Enid living like an invalid!"

"Just give her time," Todd had said soothingly, putting his arms around her and kissing the top of her head. But Elizabeth could tell that Todd was worried, too.

"Have some salad, George," Elizabeth suggested now, passing the bowl around the table.

"I can't tell you how wonderful all this is," Enid repeated. "I feel so spoiled," she added, smiling shyly at George across the table. "Liz, I must be the luckiest girl in the whole world! George has been so wonderful to me. He won't let me go anywhere by myself, and he's always jumping up to get things for me. Aren't you, George?" she prompted.

"Yeah," George mumbled. "I guess so."

Elizabeth blushed, staring down at the table. She didn't like the sound of Enid's voice at all. She just didn't sound like herself. She seemed overly cheerful, as if she were forcing herself to believe everything was all right.

"How's the physical therapy going?" Elizabeth asked gently.

Enid played with her spaghetti for a long time before answering. "Oh, all right," she said at last. "I didn't go today. I was feeling kind of tired. But tomorrow—"

"But don't you have to go?" Todd interrupted. "I thought—"

"The nurses are really strict," Enid complained. "I feel like they expect me just to jump out of the chair and run the hundred-yard dash or something. Dr. MacGregor *said* it might take me a while," she explained.

Todd and Elizabeth exchanged worried glances.

"But you can feel things in your legs now, can't you?" Elizabeth asked.

Enid sighed. "Yes, but I'm awfully weak, Liz. I shouldn't push myself too much right at the start." She stared down at her food, which she had barely tasted. "And I still can't walk," she admitted. "I've tried, but I just can't seem to do it."

"Hey," George interrupted, obviously trying to change the subject. "Did you see the baseball game on TV last night, Todd? I thought they looked really good."

Elizabeth listened as Todd chimed in with his views on how the baseball season was shaping up. But her mind wasn't really on what he was saying. She was watching Enid, wondering what she was feeling. Elizabeth knew Enid too well to fall for the act she was putting on. She could tell something was wrong, and she couldn't wait till she could get Enid alone to ask her some questions.

"What's new at school?" Enid asked later, when Elizabeth brought out the chocolate brownies she'd baked for dessert.

"Oh, the usual," Elizabeth said lightly. "Jessica's over at Cara's tonight," she added. "She's still really obsessed with her gourmet class. I think she's planning on asking the teacher to go with her to the dance next week." She giggled.

Enid glanced across the table at George, who was still deep in conversation with Todd. "I think the dance sounds like a lot of fun," she said brightly. "Maybe George and I can make it."

"I hope so," Elizabeth said quietly. "It wouldn't be any fun without you there, Enid."

For the next hour conversation ranged from pro baseball to the sale at Lisette's. Elizabeth leaned back in her chair, watching the faces around her as her friends talked, and wondered why she felt as if something were missing. It was true that everyone was being careful not to bring up any subject that might be painful. Enid didn't mention the hospital or physical therapy again, and Elizabeth felt as if they were all tiptoeing around issues that might be embarrassing or sensitive.

But that, she realized, wasn't what was making the evening so awkward. It was Enid and George.

Even if Elizabeth hadn't known George's real feelings, she could have guessed something was wrong from his behavior. Every so often he looked furtively at his watch, and once she noticed that he was drumming his fingers anxiously on the table. Elizabeth didn't think he was bored so much as nervous. He didn't look directly at Enid, either.

And Enid seemed all too aware that things

were not quite right. She was handling the embarrassing situation by pretending it wasn't there—talking louder than usual, laughing very hard at George's jokes, and all in all trying to convince the others that everything was fine.

By the time Elizabeth was clearing the coffee cups from the table, she could feel the strain in the room. The tension in the air was so thick she could almost cut it with a knife, she thought unhappily. After a silence that felt interminable, George spoke up.

"Hey," he said, "I hate to break up the party, but I have an early morning tomorrow."

"But, George—" Enid began, crestfallen.

"Maybe Liz and Todd can give you a lift home," George suggested. "That way you don't have to leave early, too."

"We'd be happy to," Elizabeth said awkwardly, "unless—"

Enid stared glumly at her plate, not saying a word.

"That's terrific, Liz," George said gratefully. "And thanks so much for dinner. It was wonderful."

The silence that fell after George left was so oppressive Elizabeth couldn't bear it. "I'm really sorry, Liz," Enid mumbled at last. It was obvious that she was deeply hurt by George's behavior, and terribly ashamed. "He's just had a lot on his mind lately. He didn't mean to be rude."

"He wasn't rude, Enid," Elizabeth said gently. "And it's kind of nice getting to be alone with you for a change. Why don't the three of us go into the living room and watch a video?"

Enid shook her head, her green eyes filling with tears. "Actually, I'm kind of tired," she murmured. "Would you think it was awful if I asked you to take me home now? I should've gone with George," she added hastily, "but I guess he thought I'd want to stay for a while. I seem to get so tired lately."

"My car's right outside," Todd volunteered. "Just tell me when, and I'm ready to go."

"Maybe right now would be best," Enid whispered. "I really do feel awfully beat."

Elizabeth thought about the dirty dishes piled up in the kitchen. It was a hard-and-fast rule in the Wakefield household that no one leave the kitchen without cleaning up. And Elizabeth's spaghetti sauce had really made a mess of her mother's pot.

"I'll come with you guys," she announced, opening the front hall closet to get her jacket. If *Mom and Dad get back before I do, I'm sure they'll understand*, she assured herself.

"Now, how do I move you in this thing?" Todd asked with a grin, trying to make Enid smile.

It didn't work. Enid looked listless and depressed, and Elizabeth had a feeling that nothing she or Todd could do would cheer her up.

George was the only one who could do that. And from the way George had bolted after dinner, it didn't look as if he was capable of keeping up the act much longer.

"Chicken cordon bleu," Jessica said dreamily, rolling over on her unmade bed to make a note next to the open cookbook. *No, maybe I should do something with beef*, she thought anxiously. *Dad's so big on steak—maybe filet mignon.*

It was funny, Jessica reflected. A couple of weeks ago she couldn't have imagined coming home before eleven on a Friday night to look through cookbooks. And that night she hardly could wait to leave Cara's and get back home.

Jessica hugged herself with satisfaction, looking happily around at the room the rest of the family had declared a natural disaster. "The Hershey Bar," Elizabeth called it, because Jessica had painted the walls chocolate brown. *But what does Elizabeth know*, Jessica thought defensively. *This room is really cozy. It's true that it's not exactly tidy.*

Even Jessica had to admit she was casual about where her clothes landed when she took them off. But Jessica loved it just as it was. She could just imagine how this room would look in *People* magazine when she became a world-famous chef. "At home," she said aloud, posing on her bed, "the artist usually spends Friday evenings thumbing through new recipes—that is, when she's not out dancing with her talented boyfriend, Jean-Pierre Baptiste."

Jessica had decided it was time to ask Jean-Pierre to go to the dance with her next Friday night. True, it was only a high school dance, and it wasn't even going to be at the country club—just in the gymnasium. But it was one of the biggest dances of the year. She was dying to go, and the obvious solution was to get Jean-Pierre to be her date. That way she could enjoy the dance *and* make Lila and Cara so jealous they'd die. *I'll ask him on Monday,* Jessica promised herself, turning back to the cookbook.

Mom and Dad's anniversary was still two weeks away, Jessica reminded herself. She was sure that by then she'd be able to make something exotic. She wrinkled her nose, looking at the recipes in the first part of the book. "Cold pumpkin soup?" she said aloud, shaking her head. "Dad wouldn't get near that for anything."

Jessica was excited about the surprise dinner for her parents. For once, she told herself triumphantly, she was going to be the good daughter. Lying back on her bed and closing her eyes, she imagined the expressions of love and joy on her parents' faces as she led them into the dining room. "Dinner is served," she would say, clapping her hands—and instantly the table would be spread with exotic dishes—chicken cordon bleu, filet mignon, veal piccatta . . .

And Elizabeth, Jessica daydreamed happily, would have been so wrapped up in Enid that she'd have forgotten all about their anniversary.

She wouldn't have bought them a single thing. And no matter what they said she'd feel absolutely terrible. Jessica would have to pretend Elizabeth helped her make something really easy, like the rice. But they'd know she had really done it all. And Elizabeth would feel like a jerk—

"Jessica!" her mother's voice interrupted her reverie. "Jessica Wakefield, are you in there?"

Jessica sat up in confusion, listening to the angry knocking on her bedroom door. "Of course I'm in here!" she shouted.

"Since when," Mrs. Wakefield inquired, opening the door and coming into the room, "do you leave a pile of dirty dishes in the sink and not even bother to *rinse* them? Do you realize that your father and I have had a long day and the last thing we want to find when we come home this late is a filthy mess in the kitchen?"

"But, Mom," Jessica said indignantly, "I didn't—"

"Don't interrupt," Mr. Wakefield echoed. "Your mother is right, Jessica. We agreed to let you take cooking classes, but we *didn't* agree to let you turn our kitchen into a demolition derby!"

"It wasn't me!" Jessica wailed, anguished. "I've been at Cara's all night! I just got home a few minutes ago, and I didn't even *go* in the kitchen."

"Oh, that's right," Mrs. Wakefield said, blinking. "Liz had Enid over to dinner. I'd forgotten."

"Foiled again," Mr. Wakefield said. "Sorry, Jess. Your middle-aged parents are getting senile early."

Mrs. Wakefield sighed. "I wonder why Liz left a mess. Did you see her, Jess, or did she just—"

"I don't know where she is," Jessica said, genuinely upset. "I can't believe you'd just assume any mess around this place is my fault."

"Sorry," Mrs. Wakefield said lightly. "Don't look so upset, Jess." She laughed. "It's hard keeping track of things when you have twins."

"I bet it is," Jessica said sulkily. "I just bet. If *I'd* made a mess down there, no one would have accused Liz."

"That isn't true, Jess," Mrs. Wakefield protested. "I'll have a word with Liz when she gets home," she added, stepping back out into the hall. "But I'm sure there's a logical explanation."

Of course there is, Jessica thought nastily. *Because it's Elizabeth. If it were me, you'd be ready to have me hung.*

"While we're on the subject of demoliton derbies," Mr. Wakefield joked, "maybe it's time you did something to this room, Jess."

Jessica didn't answer. *I'll show them*, she thought bitterly, turning back to her recipes. *I'll make them the best dinner they've ever eaten, and they'll be so sorry they insulted me they'll just beg me to forgive them.*

"Filet mignon," Jessica wrote in her notebook, trying not to feel hurt. That would teach them. She was sick and tired of being the one everyone picked on!

Eight

It was Sunday afternoon, and Enid was sitting in the Rollinses' living room in her wheelchair, leafing absently through the latest issue of *Cosmopolitan*. She barely noticed what she was looking at. It was one-thirty, and George had promised he'd come over around one.

Of course, he didn't suggest it, Enid reminded herself, frowning. *It was my idea. But I haven't seen him since Friday night, and that was such a disaster.*

Enid sighed. She hated to admit it to herself, but George had been acting strangely since the accident. He just didn't seem like himself. He kept making excuses not to see her, and when they *were* together, he didn't really look at her.

And he hasn't kissed me, she reminded herself. *Not once all week.*

"How To Tell If He Doesn't Love You Anymore," the article she'd opened to was titled. Enid bit her lip and flipped forward quickly to the color spread on bathing suits. *It's not that*, she told herself. *Of course he still loves me! He's probably just feeling strange because of everything that's happened.*

Enid could no longer pretend that something wasn't wrong. But she told herself that George still felt guilty. *He probably thinks all this is his fault*, she thought, looking down at her wheelchair.

Enid knew this was probably all the more reason to concentrate on getting better. But her heart wasn't in it. She was going to her physical therapy classes, but she just couldn't do the exercises the nurses suggested. She felt so tired all the time, and it seemed like an enormous effort just to roll the wheelchair from one side of the room to another. "I don't think I'll ever get better," Enid whispered to herself. She was afraid to say so to her mother, but she couldn't imagine being able to walk again. It seemed impossible, like something in a dream.

"Enid, George is here," Mrs. Rollins called, coming into the living room.

Enid looked up, her face brightening expectantly. "Hi," she said shyly. "How've you been, stranger? I haven't seen you all weekend!"

"I know," George mumbled, staring at the floor. "How are you?" he asked. "Any chance of getting you out of that chair today?"

Mrs. Rollins left the room, an anxious expression on her face, and Enid sighed, slowly shaking her head. "I don't think so, George," she said carefully. "I still feel awfully weak."

"Oh, well," George said, sinking down on the couch. They looked at each other, and Enid racked her brain for something to say that sounded natural. But she couldn't think of anything. She hadn't gone back to school, and all she'd really been doing that day was sitting around waiting for him to come over. She couldn't exactly tell him *that*, could she?

"Hey, I wanted to ask you about the dance on Friday," she began. "Do you want to go?"

George was quiet for a minute. "Do you think you'll feel up to it?" he asked her.

Enid bit her lip. "I hope so," she told him. "Even though I can't dance, it still sounds like fun," she added wistfully. "We've always had such a good time together at dances, George. Remember that time—"

But George didn't look as if he wanted to get nostalgic about anything. "If you want to, we can go," he said. "Whatever you want, Enid."

Enid felt like crying. This wasn't the response she'd hoped for at all. What had happened to the old George who got so excited at the thought of an evening out together? Why was he acting so cold, so distant?

"George," she whispered, reaching out to him, "is anything wrong?"

George shook his head. "No. I'm fine," he insisted. "Why?"

"I don't know," Enid mumbled. "I thought you were angry with me about something."

"Of course not!" George burst out. "How could I be angry with you?"

"I don't know," Enid repeated. "But, George, it scares me so much when you don't come by to see me. I don't know what I'd do without you. You're just about all I've got left now," she cried desperately.

George flushed deeply. "Don't say that," he said angrily. "You've got a lot more than me going for you!"

But Enid was shaking her head. "No, George, I haven't," she told him. "You're my whole world. I don't know what would happen to me if you—if you—"

"Don't," George begged her, dropping to his knees and putting his arms around her. "I can't stand it!"

Enid pulled George to her, tears falling from her eyes as she buried her face in his dark hair. *I don't know what's going on, but I feel as though I'm losing him,* she thought. *And I can't—I just can't—let him get away.*

I've just got to make him realize how much I need him, Enid told herself. *I have to make him understand that if he didn't love me anymore, I might just not be able to go on.*

Enid didn't consider whether or not she was being fair to George. She couldn't. All she knew was that she loved him and that he was drifting away from her. And if she didn't hang on for dear life, she might lose him. That was something Enid wasn't going to let happen, whatever it took.

And Enid had a feeling it was going to take everything she had—perhaps even more.

"Today, class, we graduate to the entree," Jean-Pierre announced.

"And today I'm going to graduate right out of this miserable class," Lila hissed, rolling up her sleeves. "I mean it, Jess. I've had it. Not even a sexy French accent is worth ruining two silk blouses for."

Jessica shrugged. "Go ahead and drop out if you like, Lila. But just see how far you get when you have to entertain important people one day."

"That's what servants are for." Lila giggled. "And they even do the dishes!" She eyed the uncooked chicken in front of her with distaste.

"Lila, how do I look?" Jessica asked. She had more important things on her mind than whether or not Lila stayed in the class.

"Like the Pillsbury Dough boy," Lila snorted. "You've got flour on your nose, and that apron makes you look weird."

"No, really," Jessica insisted. "I'm serious. Do I look OK?"

Lila sighed. "You look the way you always look. Gorgeous."

"Thanks," Jessica said happily. "You're such a good friend, Lila."

"Why the insecurity complex today?" Lila demanded.

Jessica lowered her voice. "I think today's the day," she confided. "I'm going to stay after class and see if Jean-Pierre wants to go the dance with me Friday night."

Lila's eyebrows shot up. "Are you really serious about that? Don't you think he's a little old for a high school dance?"

"Well, it isn't as if he'd just be going with *anyone*," Jessica pointed out. "He's probably got a real thing for American girls. Frenchmen always do in movies. Besides, haven't you noticed the way he looks at me?"

"Somehow I missed it," Lila drawled. "Good luck," she added, taking her apron off and throwing it onto the counter. "I think I've just touched my last raw chicken."

"You're not leaving now, are you?" Jessica asked, horrified.

"I certainly am," Lila told her. "You can just stay here and play kitchen with Maurice or Matisse or whatever his name is until you die, but *I've* had enough!"

Lila just didn't recognize a good thing when she saw it, Jessica thought sadly. She'd had her chance to witness the birth of the romance of the century, and she'd missed it now. But that was her problem.

Jessica took as long as she could to put her equipment away when the class was over. One by one the other students wandered out the door until only Jessica was left. Jessica, that is, and Jean-Pierre.

She had never seen the instructor look quite so handsome as he did that day. Flashing Jessica a smile, he said, "You're a fine beginning chef, Jessica. How would you like to enroll in the intermediate section?"

"I'd love to," Jessica said happily, taking her apron off. *Here it comes*, she told herself. *Now's the moment when he takes a second look at me and realizes that his prize student is actually a beautiful young woman. And then . . .*

Suddenly, the door to the classroom opened, and a redhead burst into the room, tucking her blouse into her jeans. "Jean-Pierre!" she cried. "I'm so sorry I'm late!"

To Jessica's dismay, the beautiful girl dashed to the front of the room and engulfed Jean-Pierre in a warm hug.

"Hey!" Jean-Pierre laughed, disentangling himself. "My student," he explained, pointing to Jessica.

"But I haven't seen you all *day*," the girl complained sulkily. Her accent was almost as thick as Jean-Pierre's, and Jessica, her heart sinking, had to admit she was breathtakingly beautiful.

"Jessica, this is Lizbette," Jean-Pierre said, "my wife."

"Your—" Jessica's mouth fell open. *Oh, Lord,* she thought. *Have I ever botched things up this time!* She nodded and smiled at the redhead. Then she turned to Jean-Pierre. "Thanks for the lesson," she said hastily, gathering her things together and hurrying to the door.

"See you Wednesday!" Jean-Pierre called. Jessica hurried down the corridor of the civic center, her face burning. She could still hear Lizbette's infectious laughter. *Thank goodness I didn't make a fool out of myself by asking him to the dance*, Jessica thought. *And he looked so—so—unmarried!*

Well, she wasn't going to let it get to her, she vowed, jumping into the Fiat and slamming the door. She'd still learn to be a good cook, even if it meant having to stare at Jean-Pierre knowing he was married.

It would be worth it, she told herself, to prove to her parents that for once in her life she could do something better than Elizabeth. And Jean-Pierre, or no Jean-Pierre, she was going to do it.

Wednesday afternoon Elizabeth convinced Jessica to let her take the car after school so she could go over to Enid's.

Elizabeth was more worried than ever about her friend. She still hadn't come back to school, and although she was making up assignments at home, it looked as if she was falling rapidly behind. Elizabeth had been phoning her every night, but she still felt distant from Enid, as if something were standing between them.

"I think Enid's depressed," Elizabeth told Todd, standing at his locker. "She's just not acting like herself. She doesn't seem interested in anything, she's barely eating, and she keeps complaining she's tired all the time."

"Maybe it's just the aftereffects of the accident and the operation," Todd suggested. "After all, she's been through a lot. It may just take her a little while longer, Liz."

"I wish I believed that, Todd," Elizabeth said, "but I think it's more complicated than that."

"What do you mean?" Todd asked.

"Well," Elizabeth said thoughtfully, "I think it has something to do with George. I'm not sure how it all fits together yet, but I'm sure that Enid senses something is wrong between them. She keeps trying to act like there isn't, but I can still see it in her eyes. Maybe . . ."

"What?" Todd prompted her.

"Nothing," Elizabeth said slowly. "Just a hunch. But I'm going to do what I can to cheer her up. I promised her I'd help her pick a dress to wear to the dance Friday night."

"You're going shopping?" Todd asked, surprised. "Enid can't even make it to school!"

Elizabeth laughed. "We're looking in her closet, silly," she told him. "Besides, didn't you hear? She's coming back to school on Monday. Dr. MacGregor said it'll be good for her. I think *he's* afraid she's depressed, too."

"Well, if anyone can cheer her up, you can." Todd grinned and dropped a kiss on the tip of her nose. "You sure cheer *me* up!"

Elizabeth laughed, but she felt serious as she pulled up in front of Enid's house fifteen minutes later. She wanted to help her friend so badly, but she wasn't sure how.

Enid was in her bedroom, looking critically at two dresses spread out on her bed. "Hi, Liz," she said. "Which do you think is better? I like the white one, but maybe the blue—"

"They're both beautiful," Elizabeth assured her. "Maybe the blue one," she added thoughtfully, touching the material with one hand. "It's such a nice fabric."

"Look!" Enid said, motoring herself across the room and back in her wheelchair. "I got a new wheelchair at physical therapy today. I can power this one myself. Now I don't need anyone to push me around!"

"You won't be needing it much longer anyway," Elizabeth said briskly, picking up the blue dress and admiring it. "I expect to see you dancing in George's arms Friday night."

Enid's face fell. "I hope it'll be OK," she said hollowly. "Liz, would it be OK if we doubled with you and Todd?"

"Sure," Elizabeth said, surprised. "I don't see why not. But I thought—"

"You know, George has been under a lot of pressure," Enid said conversationally. "He doesn't like to talk about it, but I think he's scared to death that the Federal Aviation Administration is going to take away his license. After all, he's wanted to be a pilot since he was a kid.

It's only natural he'd be kind of nervous lately, kind of—"

Elizabeth didn't know what to say. Her anger had cooled down a great deal since the operation, and lately she couldn't help sympathizing with George a little. *I wonder if it wouldn't almost be better for Enid if she knew the truth*, Elizabeth mused. *Not that I'd ever tell her, but as it is—*

"Oh, Liz," Enid cried, her face crumpling. "Sometimes lately I've had the feeling that George hates me because of the accident! If I hadn't begged him to take me up, it would never have happened. He'd still have his license, and—"

Enid began sobbing. Elizabeth ran to her, bending over to put her arms around her. "Don't be silly," she cried. "Of course he doesn't hate you! Oh, Enid, how could you possibly blame yourself?"

Enid lifted her face and wiped the tears from her eyes. "It's just that he's acting so different lately. I've tried and tried to find out what's bothering him, but nothing I say seems to get through to him!"

Elizabeth stared at her, dumbstruck. *If only I could tell her the truth*, she thought miserably. *If only she could forget about George and concentrate on getting out of this wheelchair!*

But Elizabeth knew it wasn't her place to tell Enid anything. All she could do was try to comfort her. Sooner or later Enid would find out the truth, but she was going to have to do it on her own.

And at this point, Elizabeth had no idea whether her friend would be strong enough to recover without George's support.

Nine

Jessica had never seen the gym look as beautiful as it did on Friday night. The dance committee had decorated it with fresh flowers, and The Droids, Sweet Valley High's own rock group, were playing up on a platform at one end of the room. School spirit was very much in display, and Jessica was determined to have a wonderful time.

It wasn't so bad, she told herself, not being there with Jean-Pierre. Her date was Ken Matthews, blond, clean-cut, and undeniably one of the cutest and most popular guys at school. Ken was captain of the football team, and even if he wasn't as sexy and mysterious as Jean-Pierre, he was a good dancer and a lot of fun at parties.

And Jessica was in her element. She knew she looked her best. Her blond hair was gleaming around her shoulders, and her cream-colored dress showed off the tan she'd labored over. And Ken—sweet, if a bit dull—had bought her a rose to pin on her dress. It smelled heavenly, and Jessica felt wonderful. She could hardly wait to start dancing.

But first Jessica wanted to get a good look at the rest of her classmates. "Let's get something to drink," she told Ken, heading in the direction of the refreshment table in one corner of the gym.

"Hey, look at that," Ken said, stopping and nudging Jessica. He pointed across the gym at Mr. Collins, the handsome English teacher who was chaperoning the dance. Mr. Collins was the best-liked teacher at Sweet Valley. Not only did he look like Robert Redford, with strawberry blond hair and laughing blue eyes, but his easy-going personality had won him quite a few admirers among the student body.

Elizabeth was one of his greatest fans, having gotten to know him quite well from working on *The Oracle*, the student newspaper for which Mr. Collins was faculty adviser.

That night Mr. Collins looked even more dashing than usual in a white linen jacket and navy-blue trousers. That wasn't what caught Ken's attention, however. Ken was pointing at Mr. Collins's dance partner, Nora Dalton, the beautiful young French teacher. "Looks like that's getting pretty serious, don't you think?" Ken chuckled.

"Maybe," Jessica said offhandedly. *I'll bet Lila's glad to see that*, she thought. Everyone knew that Nora Dalton had been dating Lila's father off and on this past winter, and Lila hadn't like it one bit. Now it looked as if things were finished between Nora Dalton and George Fowler for good. The pretty young French teacher seemed to have turned her interests elsewhere. *Ken's right*, Jessica told herself. *Just look at the way they're dancing! It's obvious they're falling in love.*

But Jessica had more important things to look at right now. "Who's Robin Wilson with?" she asked, catching sight of the brunette, who was wearing a purple dress. *She really looks like she's gained some weight*, Jessica thought critically.

"Some guy from L.A.," Ken replied. "His name is Stan, or something. I heard Robin had a hard time getting a date and this guy turned up at the last minute. He's a friend of her cousin's, or something."

"Hmmm," Jessica said thoughtfully. Stan didn't look very promising to her. He wore thick glasses, and he kept looking around the room as if he were really bored. Robin, too, kept sneaking little glances around the room. Looking for George, no doubt, Jessica concluded.

"I'll get the drinks," Ken volunteered. "What do you want?"

Jessica snapped out of her reverie. "I'd love a Coke," she told him.

As Ken hurried away, Lila came up to Jessica. "What happened to Jean-Pierre?" Lila demanded, frowning at Ken's back. "Don't tell me your little scheme backfired, Jess."

"Oh, he's way too old for me," Jessica said airily. "I wasn't really serious about him anyway, Lila. Ken's much more fun."

"I'll bet." Lila snorted.

"What about you?" Jessica asked her. "Who are you here with?"

"Someone you don't know," Lila said moodily. "His name is Louis Scott. And just between us, Jess, I don't see how I'm going to make it through the night! He's a sophomore at Sweet Valley College, and all he wants to talk about is business classes. What a bore! And he almost broke my foot the one time we danced!"

"Speaking of broken feet," Jessica whispered, her eyes glued to the main door of the gymnasium, "look who's coming."

The door to the gym had swung open, and Elizabeth and Todd came in, holding hands. Behind them, George Warren was walking beside Enid in her wheelchair. The whole gym seemed to hush as they entered, and Enid, white-faced, stared straight ahead of her as George pushed her forward.

"How inappropriate," Lila said coldly. "Who'd ever *dream* of showing up at a dance in a wheelchair! What does she think she's going to do all night?"

"Probably keep an eye on George." Jessica giggled.

"Well, she's not the only one," Lila replied. "Look at Robin Wilson."

Robin, her face flaming, was watching the foursome enter. It was clear who she was staring at, and the expression on her face gave Jessica the shivers.

She'd never seen a girl look so hopelessly in love. Then Jessica looked over at George. There was no denying the anguished look on his face as he and Robin locked gazes.

Jessica had a feeling there was going to be trouble that night.

Enid couldn't remember ever feeling as self-conscious as she did the moment the gym doors swung open and she directed her wheelchair into the crowded dance. Everyone seemed to be staring at her, and even the hours of careful preparation that afternoon didn't make her feel more self-assured. "I must look like a real idiot," she whispered to Elizabeth. "Who ever heard of a cripple coming to a dance?"

"Enid Rollins," Elizabeth snapped, "you are not a cripple! And you don't look one bit foolish. You have as much right to be here as anyone else does."

Elizabeth always knew how to make her feel better, Enid thought gratefully. But Elizabeth couldn't be expected to spend the whole night standing around consoling her. She'd come here to have fun, too. And it was enough, Enid reflected, that Elizabeth and Todd had agreed to double with her and George. Enid couldn't pre-tend any longer that the two of them were acting like a couple in love. George was so strained and uncomfortable that Enid was embarrassed in front of her friends. She was almost relieved when Todd asked Elizabeth to dance.

Almost—but not quite. Alone with George, Enid found she had absolutely nothing to say. She felt miserable.

"Why don't I get us something to drink?" he said after an uncomfortable silence.

"Go ahead," Enid told him. "I promise not to run away," she joked. She wasn't suprised when George didn't laugh.

"Enid!" a feminine voice called. And suddenly Enid was surrounded. Caroline Pearce, Olivia Davidson, DeeDee Gordon—a whole group of girls gathered around her, asking her questions and moaning with sympathy about the wheelchair. Enid found it harder than she'd expected to make small talk. Where was George? she wondered. He seemed to be taking an awfully long time getting drinks.

Suddenly she saw him through the crowd that had surrounded her. He was standing at the refreshment bar, his back to her, gesturing earnestly as he talked to someone—who was it?—a dark-haired girl in a purple dress, who was gesturing frantically back at him.

It was Robin Wilson, Enid realized, a sickening feeling in the pit of her stomach. What had she heard lately about Robin? Something about breaking up with Allen Walters because of some other guy. No one knew who it was. . . .

Robin was taking flying lessons with George,

Enid remembered suddenly. But George wouldn't— It couldn't possibly be George! It was just a coincidence, Enid assured herself. They were probably talking about the accident.

But she couldn't shake off the terrible feeling that had overcome her, not even when George came back with the drinks and tried to talk to Olivia and DeeDee.

George and Robin, she thought weakly. It just couldn't be. But, in a terrible way, it made sense.

I'm getting paranoid, Enid told herself as the group around them scattered. *I'm just feeling strange because of everything that's happened. George still loves me. He just feels guilty about the accident. And I'm so sensitive now that I'm blowing everything out of proportion. I've got to act as though it's OK.*

"You shouldn't just be standing around," she chided George, trying to make her voice sound natural. "Why don't you ask someone to dance?"

"No," George told her, shaking his head. "I'm fine, Enid. I'll just stay here with you."

"Come on!" Enid urged him desperately. "It's a dance, George. You're supposed to have fun."

"Well . . . " George said slowly. "You really won't mind, Enid? Maybe I'll just dance once."

Of course I mind! Enid thought hysterically. *I want you to stay right here with me!*

But she'd sworn to herself that she was going to act as though everything were perfectly fine. Maybe he'd ask Liz to dance, she thought. That would be OK.

103

But Elizabeth was coming over to her now as George headed back to the refreshment bar. "Enid!" Elizabeth called, "Where's George?"

Enid shook her head, tears filling her beautiful green eyes. "I made him go dance with someone," she mumbled dully, unable to keep up a brave face.

"Oh." Elizabeth stopped short. "Well, that's probably a good idea," she said cheerfully. "Are you having fun?"

"Oh, Liz," Enid cried, her face falling. "I don't know what's wrong, but George is acting so weird lately! He barely listens to anything I say, and—"

Her voice broke off in midsentence. There was no point in going any further. Enid had just seen George step onto the dance floor. The gym had darkened for a slow dance, and it was hard to see at first whom he was with.

But Enid had seen the flash of purple silk beside him, and there was no point in fooling herself a second longer. George was dancing with Robin Wilson, his arm tight around her, her head resting dreamily on his shoulder.

Elizabeth gasped, staring at her friend's stricken expression. "Are you all right?" she asked.

But Enid couldn't say a word. She just stared at the dance floor, the color draining from her face. She was *not* all right, as a matter of fact. And she had a terrible feeling she was never going to be all right again.

*　　*　　*

"Oh, Todd, it was just terrible," Elizabeth cried. "You should have seen her face!"

Elizabeth told him the whole story. After George had left the dance floor, he returned to Enid. And Enid had blown up, right in front of Elizabeth. "You're in love with Robin Wilson, aren't you?" she demanded.

"What did George say?" Todd asked.

Elizabeth shook her head. "You know, Todd, I felt kind of bad for him. I could tell he wanted to keep from hurting Enid, but the truth was written all over his face. And he looked so relieved to have it out in the open at last."

"What about Enid?" Todd went on, "Was she OK?"

Elizabeth shook her head sadly. "I don't think so," she told him. "She looked completely devastated. George never answered her question, but he didn't have to. His face gave it all away. And Enid could barely talk, she was so upset. She just told him she wanted to go home. And as they were leaving, I saw her face just completely crumple. She was crying her heart out."

"Maybe you should go over and see her later tonight," Todd suggested. "She'll probably need a good friend's shoulder to cry on."

"I don't think so," Elizabeth said. "I think she may want to be alone tonight. But I'll go see her tomorrow."

Elizabeth couldn't take her mind off Enid for the rest of the evening. As hard as she tried, she couldn't enjoy the dance. All she could think about was the look on Enid's face when she'd spotted George and Robin in each other's arms. What if that ever happened to Todd? Elizabeth wondered unhappily. What would she do without him?

But she couldn't picture Todd falling in love with someone else. It seemed impossible. But then, Enid must have felt the same way once.

As always, Todd seemed to be reading her mind. "Come dance with me," he urged her, taking her in his arms. "Liz, I don't know what I'd do without you," he whispered in her ear when they were out on the dance floor. "Don't you go getting any silly ideas in your head about some other guy."

"Oh, Todd," Elizabeth murmured, tightening her arms around him. *I'm so lucky*, she told herself. *So incredibly lucky to have a guy like Todd in love with me.*

"How would you like to go out to dinner with me tomorrow night?" Todd asked Elizabeth, stroking her blond hair with his hand. "I was thinking of someplace really special, like The Palomar House."

"But that place costs a fortune!" Elizabeth gasped. "What's the occasion?"

"How quickly they forget," Todd said sadly, the twinkle in his eye showing Elizabeth he was only kidding. "Our monthly anniversary, of course," he said grandly.

"Anniversary!" Elizabeth gasped. "Oh, Todd,

I completely forgot about my parents' wedding anniversary! It's next Friday, and I don't have anything planned for them!"

"Why don't you buy them tickets to the dinner-theater show at Bayside?" Todd suggested. "I did that for my parents last year, and they really loved it."

"What a wonderful guy you are," Elizabeth said happily. "That's a brilliant idea! They'll be really surprised."

"That still doesn't settle the question of *our* anniversary," Todd said huskily, drawing her back into his arms.

"Your wish is my command." Elizabeth laughed and rested her head against his strong chest. It was so wonderful to be in Todd's arms that despite herself Elizabeth began to relax and enjoy the music.

But she couldn't quite put the thought of Enid out of her mind. How was Enid taking tonight's events, she wondered—and what effect would her realization about George have on her recovery?

Only time would tell, Elizabeth thought uneasily. It was going to take a lot of strength for Enid to get back on her feet without George there to cheer her on. She hoped Enid was strong enough.

Ten

As it turned out, Elizabeth didn't have a chance to be alone with Enid until Sunday afternoon. Enid was out when Elizabeth dropped by on Saturday. Her mother had taken her to the hospital for physical therapy. And when Elizabeth called her later in the afternoon, Mrs. Rollins said she was napping.

Enid was awake when Elizabeth went by on Sunday. She was sitting on the Rollins's porch in her wheelchair, working on some makeup assignments for Mr. Collins. She barely looked up when Elizabeth plopped into a chair beside her.

"I've been so worried about you," Elizabeth began. "Enid, tell me what happened when George took you home Friday night."

"Friday night?" Enid said blankly. "What do you mean?"

"Well, you know," Elizabeth began awkwardly. "After the whole thing about Robin Wilson."

"Robin doesn't mean a thing to George," Enid said coolly. "It was just a big misunderstanding."

Elizabeth eyebrows shot up. "But I thought—"

"Well, you were wrong," Enid continued. "After all, I told him to dance with someone. And Robin wasn't dancing with anyone."

"Oh," Elizabeth said blankly. She didn't know what else to say. Enid wasn't even looking at her, but she could tell her friend was holding something in. Her face was very pale, and she had shadows under her eyes, suggesting she hadn't gotten much sleep. "Then is everything OK between you and George?" she asked.

Enid shrugged. "Why shouldn't it be?"

Elizabeth couldn't bear to see her best friend shutting her out this way. She had to make Enid talk this thing out. "Have you seen George since Friday night?" she asked.

"I don't really want to talk about the whole thing, Liz," Enid remarked. "What George feels is his business. But I will say this," she added. "I know George too well to think that he'd leave me for Robin as long as I'm. . ." She looked down at her wheelchair, and her voice trailed off.

"But if he really loves Robin," Elizabeth began, "you wouldn't *want* him to stay with you, would you?"

Enid looked up at Elizabeth, her green eyes cold. "As I said, Liz, I don't know *how* George really feels. But he wouldn't stay with me if he didn't want to."

Elizabeth couldn't believe her ears. How could Enid pressure George to stay with her, knowing he was really in love with another girl? She couldn't believe Enid was really behaving this way.

"Enid, tell me how you're feeling," she pleaded. "You can't really—"

"I told you," Enid said. "George is all I've got left. You can hardly expect me just to tell him to run off and leave me here in this wheelchair, can you?"

"But—"

"Case closed," Enid said without a smile. "Liz, I appreciate your coming over, but I'm really not feeling very well. I think I'm going to go lie down and take a nap."

Elizabeth bit her lip, not knowing what to say, "How did your physical therapy class go yesterday?" she asked at last. "Did Dr. MacGregor say anything about your progress?"

"What could he say?" Enid asked sharply. "It's pretty obvious isn't it? There hasn't been any progress at all."

Elizabeth stared at her best friend, appalled by the bitterness in her voice. This wasn't the Enid Rollins she knew! What had happened to her courage, her will to get better?

"Let's face it," Enid added, powering her wheelchair to the door. "No matter what anyone says, Liz, I'm never going to walk again. I'm going to be a cripple for the rest of my life. And the sooner you and everyone else gets used to the idea, the easier it'll be!"

"It was just terrible, Jess," Elizabeth said, slumping over the counter in the Wakefield kitchen. "I couldn't believe it was Enid talking. She sounded so . . . I don't know, so caustic!"

"One pound of pasta shells," Jessica muttered under her breath, pulling her blond hair back with one hand. "The water's already boiling, a dash of salt . . . "

"You're not even listening to me!" Elizabeth cried, anguished.

"Of course I am," Jessica said soothingly. "But this part is tricky, Liz. Don't you want dinner to come out right?"

Jessica had convinced Mrs. Wakefield to let her cook dinner that night, and she wanted everything to go smoothly. It was her trial run for Friday's performance.

"What's it going to be, Jess?" Elizabeth asked suspiciously, prodding the mussels cooling off in a colander.

"A cold seafood and pasta salad," Jessica told her proudly. "It's got lots of things in it—mussels, clams, crabmeat, lobster. Jean-Pierre says it's absolutely divine."

"Does it have a name?"

"No," Jessica admitted. "It's too good for a name. Don't worry, Liz. You're going to love it."

111

"I'm really worried about Enid," Elizabeth went on. "What do you suppose is keeping her from being able to walk? The doctors promised she'd be back to her old self by now."

"Well," Jessica said philosophically, "look at it from Enid's point of view. She doesn't have much to gain from walking, does she?"

"What do you mean?" Elizabeth asked.

Jessica shrugged, taking the crabmeat out of the refrigerator and turning the water on in the sink. "From what you just told me, it sounds like Enid thinks that the minute she walks, George will start running—right in the direction of Robin Wilson."

"But Enid wouldn't deliberately pretend she couldn't walk!" Elizabeth burst out.

"Maybe not," Jessica admitted. "It was just an idea."

"I don't know." Elizabeth sighed. "The whole think is so depressing. She wouldn't even *talk* to me, Jess. She just kept acting as if everything with George is fine. And I *know* it can't be."

"Maybe Mom and Dad are right," Jessica suggested. "Maybe you just expect too much of her too quickly."

"Maybe," Elizabeth said uneasily. "But I don't think so. I think Enid is taking way too long to pull herself together."

"Speaking of pulling things together," Jessica pointed out, "I don't have much time to pull this thing together."

"I can take a hint," Elizabeth grumbled. "Does

the crab stay that color after you've cooked it?" she added dubiously, or does it get a little more pink?"

"Who's the chef around here?" Jessica demanded. "Don't worry about a thing, sister, dear. You're just going *to love it!*"

Two hours later Jessica leaned back in her chair with a satisfied smile. Her parents and Elizabeth had scraped their plates clean, and now they were sitting, having coffee. "Dinner wasn't bad, was it?" she asked anxiously. Actually, Jessica had been too busy getting things ready to do more than taste. But everyone else really seemed to enjoy the salad.

"Delicious," Mr. Wakefield said, giving Jessica a big smile. "I'm really proud of you. Though I *did* wonder why the chef didn't eat her own cooking."

"Would you excuse me?" Elizabeth said suddenly, pushing her chair back hastily. Her face had turned a funny color, and her hand was clasped over her mouth.

"What's wrong, dear?" Mrs. Wakefield asked anxiously.

Elizabeth didn't answer. She knocked her chair over in her haste to get away from the table, and the next sound the Wakefields heard was the slam of the bathroom door down the hall.

"Oh, dear," Mrs. Wakefield said, holding her stomach with one hand. "I feel a little peculiar. I wonder . . ."

"What is it?" Jessica demanded. "What's wrong with everybody?"

"Will you just excuse me?" Mrs. Wakefield said, pushing her chair back and standing up. "I feel a bit ill, I'm afraid. I'm sure it's just—"

"Jessica," Mr. Wakefield said sternly, "what did you put in that salad?"

"Clams," Jessica said nervously. "And crabmeat and a bit of lobster and mussels. I worked so hard to get them open after I cooked them."

"The mussels didn't open when you steamed them?" Mr. Wakefield demanded. Jessica shook her head. She thought he was beginning to look a little green himself. "Jess, if the shells don't open, you're not supposed to eat them." He gulped. "You can get food poisoning—"

"Maybe you'd better go to the bathroom," she suggested. "Judging from Liz and Mom, you've got about twelve seconds before—"

"Oh, God." Mr. Wakefield groaned, holding his stomach with both hands. "Jessica, what were you trying to do—poison your whole family with one blow?" He got up and quickly left the room.

Oh, no, Jessica thought miserably, sitting at the table and listlessly stirring her coffee. She'd wondered why a number of the mussels had remained closed, but she'd pried them, thinking it was a shame to throw them out when they were so expensive.

And dinner was supposed to be such a success, she

thought sadly. Instead it looked as if she had made everybody completely sick.

"Jessica Wakefield!" Elizabeth was hollering, weaving her way back into the dining room and reaching for a glass of water. "I don't know what your explanation is, but you'd better come up with one quick!"

"I was just experimenting," Jessica said, injured. "I didn't mean to—"

"Where is she?" the twins heard their mother say angrily.

"Uh-oh," Jessica said. "It sounds like Mom's sort of on the rampage."

"If I were you," Elizabeth said dryly, "I'd make myself something to eat fast. That'll finish you off, and Mom won't be able to say anything."

Jessica sighed. Dinner number one hadn't gone exactly as she'd planned. But there was still Friday, she told herself hopefully. Friday night would give her a chance to redeem herself—if tonight didn't kill her mom and dad off!

"You sound absolutely terrible!" Todd exclaimed when he got Elizabeth on the telephone later that evening. "What happened to you?"

"Jessica Wakefield," Elizabeth moaned, "is what happened to me. Todd, I think there's a future for that girl in the Department of Defense.

She's discovered something much more deadly than nuclear bombs."

"What is it?" Todd asked.

"Seafood something-or-other," Elizabeth said dramatically. "It doesn't even have a name. It must be a top secret." She couldn't help giggling as she told Todd what had happened at dinner. "We're all sick," she concluded. "All but Jess. She didn't have time to eat enough, she was so busy poisoning the rest of us!"

"Sounds like Jessica," Todd said. "But I'm glad everyone's all right. Listen, I wanted to ask you something. Did you get to see Enid today?"

"I did," Elizabeth admitted. "But it wasn't very successful." She told Todd exactly what she'd told Jessica earlier that afternoon. But Todd, unlike her twin, was concerned.

"I don't like the sound of that at all," he told her. "What do you think we can do to help her?"

"I don't know," Elizabeth said thoughtfully. "But something Jessica said this afternoon has given me an idea."

"You don't mean you want to food-poison poor Enid!" Todd laughed.

"No." Elizabeth giggled. "Far from it. I barely have a plan yet, Todd. It's all too shadowy to talk about. Would you hate me if I kept quiet about this for a few days while I think if over?"

"Of course not," Todd told her. "Are you still keeping quiet about your parents' anniversary, too?"

"You bet. I want to surprise them with the tickets."

"In that case," Todd said wryly, "you'd better keep it quiet around Jessica, too. You know how long a secret lasts with her!"

"I know," Elizabeth said. "I'm not going to tell her until I give my parents the tickets. But it's not that I don't trust her," she insisted, always defensive about her twin. "I just want Jessica to be surprised, too."

"From the way it sounds," Todd remarked, "*Jessica* deserves a surprise after what she did to you guys tonight."

"She couldn't help it." Elizabeth sighed. "And she's so upset, Todd. She really feels terrible."

"Not as bad as you guys feel, I bet!"

Elizabeth laughed, but her mind wasn't on Jessica or her family anymore. She was thinking about Enid.

Jessica just may have given me a valuable clue today, she thought. *And if her hunch proves to be right, I think I have a plan to get Enid out of that wheelchair!*

Eleven

"Elizabeth!" Mrs. Wakefield called. "Mrs. Rollins is here to see you!"

Elizabeth had been floating on a raft in the Wakefields' swimming pool, her fingers trailing in the water. Her mother's announcement surprised her so much she tipped the raft over, soaking herself completely.

"I'll be out in a minute!" she spluttered, swimming to the side of the pool and pulling herself out.

"I'll make some iced tea for you," Mrs. Wakefield was saying, leading Mrs. Rollins outside. "I'm glad I was home early today and could catch you," she added. Mrs. Wakefield didn't usually get home before dinner on Mondays, but a client had canceled his appointment, leaving her a free hour.

Elizabeth wrapped a towel around herself, then sat down in a chair next to Mrs. Rollins.

"How are you?" she asked politely. "And how's Enid? She wasn't in school today."

"No," Mrs. Rollins said. "I took her over to see Dr. MacGregor this afternoon, as a matter of fact. Liz, that's why I've come over to talk to you. I've been worried about Enid's behavior lately, and I thought you might be able to help me understand what's causing it."

"What do you mean?" Elizabeth asked evasively. She wanted nothing more than to pour her own worries out to Enid's mother, but she sensed that it might not be fair to her friend to do so.

"Well," Mrs. Rollins began, "she doesn't seem like her old self to me. I expected some adjustments would have to be made after the accident, of course. But Enid seems to have just given up. She's been very stubborn about her physical therapy classes. The nurses tell me she's made almost no progress at all. And when she's home, almost all she does is sleep. So today I took her over to see Dr. MacGregor for a complete examination."

"What did he say?"

Mrs. Rollins sighed. "He was surprised by her condition. He expected her to be much further along by now. In fact, he told me that Enid should be walking. He said that the X rays confirmed that the operation was one-hundred-percent successful. Enid's spine is in normal condition, and there's no physical reason why she isn't walking."

Elizabeth thought for a minute. "Why does Dr. MacGregor think she's still in the wheelchair?" she asked. "Did he give you any reasons?"

"Yes," Mrs. Rollins said. "He thinks she has a psychological block against recovering. He told me this is far more common that people realize. I guess the mind has mysterious powers in situations like this. It isn't that Enid knows she can walk and won't. She really believes she can't move. What we need to discover is *why* she won't let herself recover. That's why I came to see you, Liz. I know you and Enid are very close, and I thought you might have some idea of what may be troubling her."

Elizabeth bit her lip. She wanted to help Enid, but she felt that confiding in Mrs. Rollins about George wouldn't be fair. "I'm afraid I really can't help you very much," she said truthfully. "I've been worried about Enid, too. I kept feeling that she ought to be more eager to get better. And I could tell that for some reason she preferred to act as if it was all out of her hands. But I really can't tell you why she's behaving this way."

"I tried to reach George, too," Mrs. Rollins continued. "But his mother told me that he'd taken a few days off from school and gone on a camping trip. She said he wanted to be by himself for a while. The poor boy. I think all the pressure must really be getting to him."

Elizabeth didn't say anything. *I wonder if George told Enid he was going,* she mused. Elizabeth was beginning to think she had a pretty good idea why Enid wasn't allowing herself to get better. But she couldn't tell Mrs. Rollins about it. She wasn't positive, but she thought it might have something to do with George and Robin.

I wonder who I could talk to about it? she asked herself. Her parents didn't seem right.

Then she thought of Mr. Collins. He had always given her good advice in the past. Maybe she could call him and go over to his house before dinner. At least she could sound him out on the ideas she was tossing around.

Because if Enid really did have a mental block, Elizabeth told herself, she had to think of some way of helping her friend get over it. She couldn't bear to think of Enid staying in a wheelchair for the rest of her life.

"Elizabeth Wakefield!" Mr. Collins said, opening his front door. "It's good to see you. Come on in," he urged, leading the way down his front hall to the living room. "So, what can I do for you?"

"Well, I—" Elizabeth didn't get much further than that before she was accosted by Teddy, Mr. Collins's six-year-old son. Mr. Collins was divorced from his wife, and he had taken full responsibility for the adorable boy who was now hurling himself at Elizabeth's legs.

"Whoa!" Elizabeth cried, disentangling herself

and giving Teddy a huge hug. "You're getting bigger all the time," she told him, rumpling his hair.

"Nora!" Mr. Collins called. "Elizabeth Wakefield is here!"

The door to the kitchen opened, and Nora Dalton came out, a white apron over her pretty flowered dress. Elizabeth blushed. She had sensed that something was starting between Mr. Collins and Ms. Dalton, but she hadn't expected to find the pretty French teacher in Mr. Collins's home.

"Nora and I are brainstorming this afternoon," Mr. Collins told her, taking out a pipe and lighting it. "We're trying to think of a good idea for a junior class fund-raiser. What do you think, Liz? Any suggestions?"

Ms. Dalton laughed. "Liz didn't come over here to get dragged into this, Roger. Maybe you should find out why she came."

"But I'd love to help you!" Elizabeth protested.

"Another time." Mr. Collins smiled. "Ms. Dalton's right. What brings you over here, Liz? Is anything wrong?"

Elizabeth took the chair he offered her and sighed heavily. "As a matter of fact, I came to ask your advice about Enid Rollins."

"I thought that might be it," Mr. Collins said. "Still no progress, huh?"

"Dr. MacGregor thinks she has a psychological block," Elizabeth told him. "He thinks she's able to walk but just won't let herself."

"That's interesting," Mr. Collins mused. "What do you think, Liz? Any ideas on why she wouldn't want to get better?"

Taking a deep breath, Elizabeth told her favorite teacher all about George and Robin. She knew she could trust Mr. Collins, and his relaxed, friendly manner kept her from feeling silly about troubling him with this kind of problem. "Enid said something to me last week about the whole thing," she concluded. "She said George would never leave her for Robin as long as she was in this condition."

"So you think she's deliberately keeping herself from walking so she won't lose George?"

Elizabeth nodded. "Or if not deliberately, she's unconsciously doing the same thing. I think she's afraid that as soon as she's better, she won't have any hold over George. And she's afraid of what will happen when that occurs."

"I think that's very perceptive of you," Ms. Dalton said. "You've got a pretty keen understanding of human nature, Liz."

Elizabeth blushed. "Jessica gave me the idea, really," she said. "And I have to admit it seems like the most logical explanation."

"What do you think can be done for Enid?" Mr. Collins asked.

Elizabeth thought for a moment. "I've got one idea, but it's kind of a long shot," she told him. "I'd feel too stupid explaining it right now."

"Nothing wrong with that!" Mr. Collins laughed. "I feel that way about our fund-raiser right now."

"Mr. Collins," Elizabeth asked suddenly, leaning forward on her chair, "can I ask you for a huge favor?"

"Sure, Liz. What is it?"

"I don't suppose," Elizabeth began, "I could borrow Teddy one afternoon after school this week?"

"Borrow him?" Mr. Collins burst out laughing. "What do you mean?"

"You know." Elizabeth shrugged. "Bring him home with me and pretend I'm baby-sitting for him. Would that be OK?"

"You're more than welcome to," Mr. Collins told her. "I don't suppose this has anything to do with this mysterious plan of yours?"

Elizabeth smiled. "It does," she admitted. "And if I can pull this off, Teddy just may be able to help me get Enid out of that wheelchair once and for all!"

Jessica got home from her cooking class Monday just before dinner. She was still feeling sulky after what had happened the previous night. *What a bunch of ingrates*, she thought. *Can I help it if the mussels were bad? You'd think I poisoned them all on purpose!*

Cooking class had only cheered her up a little. It was the last lesson, and Jean-Pierre had handed her a diploma and given her a special smile.

"You," he told her, "are my prize student. You must come back again."

So there, Jessica thought. At least *he* didn't think she was a failure.

But not even Jean-Pierre's praise cheered her up very much. She'd heard from one of the other students in the class that Lizbette couldn't even bake brownies. *I guess he doesn't find cooking ability all that attractive in women*, Jessica thought sadly. *I should have had him over to dinner last night.*

The thing to do, Jessica told herself, was to make sure the dinner she was planning for Friday night would be perfect. She already had a revised menu planned—veal piccata, string beans, wild rice, and raspberry torte for dessert. There was no way anything in that could make them sick, she thought triumphantly. And then they'd change their minds about her cooking ability.

"Want some help with dinner?" she called to her mother, who was setting the table.

Mrs. Wakefield burst out laughing. "No, thanks," she said dryly. "I was at half-mast all day today. I think I'd better stick to chicken soup tonight."

"I couldn't help it," Jessica said indignantly. "How was I supposed to—"

"Jess," Mrs. Wakefield said fondly, "I was only teasing you. You shouldn't be so sensitive."

I'm never allowed to be the sensitive one, Jessica

thought moodily, dragging her feet as she went up to her bedroom. *It's different for Liz. Everyone expects her to be sensitive. She's the one who cares about what people say and is incredibly thoughtful all the time.*

But Friday night would change everything, she thought. Elizabeth hadn't said a word about their parents' anniversary, and Jessica was convinced she'd forgotten it. So for once, she, Jessica, would be the good, loving daughter. As far as she was concerned, she'd fouled up for the last time.

Twelve

Wednesday evening the Wakefields went out for Mexican food in downtown Sweet Valley. "Just think." Mr. Wakefield grinned. "A few nights ago I thought I'd never want to eat again, and now I'm actually looking forward to enchiladas!"

"Ha-ha-ha," Jessica said bitterly. She was sick and tired of being teased about the food-poisoning incident. Couldn't anyone in the family find anything else to talk about?

"What's wrong, Liz?" You look kind of down in the dumps," Mrs. Wakefield said, after the waiter had taken their order.

"Oh, it's nothing," Elizabeth said. "I'm just a little worried about Enid, I guess."

"Has anything changed since she saw Dr. MacGregor on Monday?"

Elizabeth shook her head. "Still the same old thing. The psychiatrist at the hospital is positive Enid has a mental block. And until she overcomes it, she won't be able to walk. But Enid refuses to talk about it with anyone. She swears she'll never get better."

"It's that jerk George Warren's fault," Jessica remarked. "She's just afraid he'll run off with Robin the minute she gets better. And I don't blame her, either. He's been seeing Robin behind Enid's back since the accident, so why *wouldn't* he run off as soon as he could manage not to look like a total bum?"

"Jessica," Mrs. Wakefield hissed. "We're in a restaurant. Can't you keep your voice down?"

"Why?" Jessica asked innocently. "I'm only telling the truth."

"How do you know George is still seeing Robin?" Mr. Wakefield asked Jessica.

"Because he *is*," Jessica said calmly. "Everyone knows it."

"But *how* does everyone know it?" Mr. Wakefield pressed her.

"Daddy, I'm not testifying in court. You don't have to look so serious."

"But it's a serious matter, Jess," her father said soberly. "Suppose someone overheard what you said about George. If it isn't true, he might accuse you of slander."

"Oh, Daddy," Jessica said, "it *is* true. Lila and I saw George's car parked in front of Robin's house the day after the accident. It was perfectly obvious what was going on!"

"I'm afraid she's right, Dad." Elizabeth sighed. "But in any case, Enid seems oblivious to the whole thing. She won't talk about it, anyway. And she refuses to admit it has anything to do with her inability to walk.''

"It's such a shame," Mrs. Wakefield said. "If it were one of you girls, I'd—well, I don't know what I'd do."

"Well, I think George is a selfish slob," Jessica announced.

"Jess," Mrs. Wakefield said warningly.

"He is!" Jessica shrieked indignantly. "How can he do this to the poor girl! I think it's horrible."

"You know," Elizabeth said thoughtfully, "a few weeks ago I would have agreed with you, Jess. But the more I've seen of the situation, the more I sympathize with George. I don't think Enid means to be manipulative, but that's just what she's being. George tried to level with her, and she refused to listen. To be honest, I feel kind of sorry for him."

"That-a-girl!" Mr. Wakefield laughed. "I knew I could count on you to be objective, Liz."

Jessica was losing her appetite. *Thanks a lot, Liz,* she thought silently. *Make me look horrible, as usual.* She shot Elizabeth her meanest scowl, but her twin wasn't paying attention.

"On a happier subject," she was saying, "you two have an anniversary coming up, don't you?" Elizabeth's blue-green eyes were twinkling.

Oh, God, Jessica thought, slumping in her chair. *Now I'm completely ruined!*

"I thought you two had forgotten!" Mrs. Wakefield said, smiling.

"I wanted to surprise you both, but I'm afraid if I wait any longer you'll make plans," Elizabeth continued, taking two tickets out of her purse. "How do you feel about a night on the town this Friday?"

"Two tickets to Bayside!" Mrs. Wakefield exclaimed. "Liz, what a wonderful idea! We haven't been there in ages. Do you remember, Ned, the wonderful dinner-theater evening they put on?"

"But I was going to surprise you with a gourmet dinner Friday night!" Jessica wailed.

Mr. and Mrs. Wakefield exchanged amused glances. "It's probably just as well." Mr. Wakefield grinned. "That's terribly sweet of you, Jess, but I'm not sure I'll be fully recovered from Sunday night by then."

Jessica's lower lip trembled. *What a bunch of jerks I've got for a family*, she thought. How could they possibly blame her for a stupid accident like that? And she'd slaved on the menu for Friday night! "It was going to be so perfect," she said mournfully, barely realizing she'd spoken aloud.

"Maybe you could make us dinner Saturday night," Mrs. Wakefield suggested, shaking her head at her husband.

"Forget it," Jessica muttered. "It wouldn't be the same."

The whole point of the dinner was ruined now. As usual, Elizabeth had come out of the whole thing smelling like a rose. And Jessica—

Well, I guess I'm just the thorn, Jessica thought miserably.

"Look, food's here," Elizabeth said brightly, hoping to change the subject.

But Jessica was still slumped in her chair, a scowl on her pretty face. "Food," she muttered, "is the last thing I want to think about for a while." She couldn't believe how disappointed she was about Friday night. And none of the others seemed to be giving it a second thought.

Jessica couldn't remember the last time she'd felt so thoroughly and devastatingly misunderstood. *I'll make it up somehow*, she promised herself. *I'll find some way to outshine Liz!*

But how?

"Robin," Elizabeth said, lowering her lunch tray, "do you mind if I join you?"

Robin Wilson looked up blankly, her blue eyes focusing on Elizabeth with surprise. "Sure," she said, waving her hand. "You're welcome, Liz."

The cafeteria was buzzing with activity, but Elizabeth barely noticed the din around her. "I've been thinking about you a lot lately," she told the girl, "and I feel I owe you a big apology for the way I acted that day at Casey's. I think I sort of flew off the handle. I thought you and George were still seeing each other, even after the crash."

"Oh, that's all right," Robin said vaguely. "I don't blame you for being mad. But you were wrong, you know," she added. "I talked to George at the dance. That was the first time I'd spoken to him since the night he called me after the accident. And it was the *only* time I've seen him since then."

Elizabeth decided she had to confront the situation; she had to learn the truth. "But Jessica said she and Lila saw George's car in front of your house the day after the plane crash."

Robin laughed bitterly. "George told me that the night of the dance. He dropped by to tell me in person what he ended up telling me over the phone—that we shouldn't see each other again. But he forgot to tell me he'd come by."

Elizabeth gasped! "Oh, Robin, I feel so foolish. Do you think you can forgive me for having been so horrible to you?"

Robin smiled. "You weren't horrible," she said. "You were just defending your best friend. Believe me, Liz, I would've done the same thing. And I don't blame you for hating me, either. But I couldn't help falling in love with George. It just happened."

"Do you still love him?" Elizabeth asked gently.

Robin sighed. "Yes," she said quietly. "But I've given up hope. As long as Enid needs him, George will stick by her. And it looks like the poor girl is going to need him for a long, long time. You know, Liz," she added, "I love George, but I care too much about my self-respect to do something rotten."

132

"How does George feel about all this?" Elizabeth asked.

Robin's eyes filled with tears. "Well"—she bit her lip—"George wants to start seeing me again now," she admitted. "He's getting fed up with Enid. He feels that she's refusing to get better so she can hang on to him. But I said I won't see him until Enid's up and walking. I can't have her misery on my conscience—not until she's well."

"You're an amazing person," Elizabeth said quietly. "I'm not sure I could be that noble if I were you."

Robin shrugged. "It doesn't have anything to do with being noble. I guess it just has to do with being able to sleep at night!"

"I just hope you can forgive me and be my friend again," Elizabeth said seriously. "I said a lot of things I shouldn't have and made a lot of quick judgments before I had reason to."

"You're just a loyal friend," Robin repeated. "Of course I forgive you, Liz. I used to wish I could be like you," she added suddenly. "And I still respect you so much. I'm glad we're friends again."

"Thanks," Elizabeth told her warmly. "I don't know about you, but I can guarantee *I'll* sleep better tonight now that we've made up!"

"I feel better, too," Robin admitted.

Now, Elizabeth thought anxiously, *I've just got to make my plan work to get Enid out of her wheelchair! Because without that, I doubt I'll ever get a good night's sleep again as long as I live.*

133

* * *

That night Elizabeth dialed Enid's number. "Enid, it's me," she said into the phone. "How are you?"

"I'm OK," Enid said unenthusiastically. "About the same. What's up?"

"I need to talk to you about something really important," Elizabeth told her. "Can you come over tomorrow afternoon?"

Enid was quiet for a minute. "Can't you talk to me about it now?"

Elizabeth dropped her voice. "It's not private enough around here," she answered.

"Oh." Enid was quiet again. "What about in school tomorrow?"

"Enid, this is *private*," Elizabeth persisted. "Please come over!"

"Oh, OK." Enid sighed. "I'll ask Mom to give me a ride over. But I promised her I'd go to the hospital after school to meet a new doctor, so I won't be able to make it till around four-thirty or so."

"That's fine," Elizabeth said. "See you then, Enid."

The minute Elizabeth hung up she dialed Mr. Collins's number.

"The mystery plan is in operation at last!" he exclaimed when he heard her voice. "And I suppose you want to recruit Boy Wonder to help you!"

Elizabeth giggled. "If Boy Wonder is around, can I talk to him for a few minutes?"

Teddy Collins was on the phone in a flash, his voice high with excitement. "OK, Liz, what's the plan?" he asked.

"You're a good swimmer, Teddy, aren't you?" Elizabeth asked him.

"The best!" Teddy chirped. "I was in the Sharks last summer at camp!"

"Good," Elizabeth said. "I thought so. How would you like to come swimming over at my house tomorrow afternoon? I'll tell you the rest of the plan then."

"Goody!" Teddy cried. "It's just like on television!"

"Now, I'll pick you up around four o'clock," Elizabeth instructed him, and you'll get your mysterious assignment. OK?"

"OK!" Teddy hollered. "I can't wait!"

Elizabeth sat still for a couple of minutes after she'd replaced the receiver, running through the plan she'd come up with for what must have been the hundredth time. It had to work, she told herself. It just had to.

She couldn't think of any way to get Enid on her feet that wasn't drastic. But Elizabeth was prepared to be drastic now. Her best friend's entire future was at stake, and Elizabeth wasn't about to let Enid just lie back and give up.

Elizabeth was going to fight for Enid's recovery with all her might. And if it meant trying a desperate trick to save her, Elizabeth figured it was well worth the attempt.

Thirteen

"OK, Teddy," Elizabeth said, dangling her feet in the swimming pool. "Have you got the plan down?"

Teddy nodded, his blue eyes twinkling. "Do you think it'll really work, Liz?"

Elizabeth sighed. "I sure hope so," she told him. Just then there was the faint sound of the front doorbell. Elizabeth quickly got up. "That must be Enid. I'll be right back, Teddy."

Several minutes later Enid had wheeled out to the patio surrounding the Wakefields' swimming pool. Late afternoon sunlight danced on the water. Standing next to Enid, Elizabeth took a deep breath, crossing her fingers behind her back. Her plan had better work, she told herself. She didn't know what she'd do if it failed.

"Now, Teddy, stay away from the edge of the pool," she warned, getting to her feet. "I'm going to go in and get us some root beer."

"Sure, Liz," Teddy called merrily, running his toy truck along the cement lip at the deep end.

"Keep an eye on him, will you, Enid?" Elizabeth said as she opened the sliding door to the house. "He can't swim," she added under her breath.

Enid's eyebrows shot up. "But, Liz—"

"I'll just be a second," Elizabeth promised.

Teddy waited until Elizabeth was safely inside before he began to put the first part of Elizabeth's plan into effect.

"Look, Enid!" he called. "I can make my truck go really fast!"

Crawling around the edge of the deep end, Teddy pushed his truck before him, moving faster and faster on the slippery cement.

"Be careful, Teddy," Enid said anxiously, leaning forward in her wheelchair. *Liz didn't tell me she was going to be baby-sitting*, she thought unhappily. *I thought she wanted to talk to me alone.*

"It's OK," Teddy assured her, backing up and running the truck in the other direction.

"I mean it, Teddy," Enid said warningly. "You're way too close to the water. Why don't you—"

But her warning was too late. The truck shot out of Teddy's hand into the deep end of the pool, and an instant later he jumped in after it, spluttering as the water came up over his head.

"Teddy!" Enid screamed. Gripping the wheelchair with both hands, she started to drive herself forward. "Liz!" she screamed at the top of her lungs. "Teddy's drowning!"

But there was no answer from inside the Wakefield house. *She can't hear me*, Enid thought desperately. Teddy was fighting to stay above the water. She could see his little body flailing helplessly as he sank once, struggled, and sank again. The next minute Enid was on her feet. Her legs felt like rubber, and her whole body ached as she stumbled forward. But she didn't care. She didn't have time to think. She just had to make it to the other side of the pool.

Within seconds she was at the opposite edge. "Hang on, Teddy. I'm coming!" she called, jumping into the water.

"Enid!" the little boy gasped, fighting for breath. "Help me!"

Enid swam to Teddy and fitted the crook of her elbow around his head, then pulled him back with her to the shallow end. Just then the sliding door opened, and Elizabeth ran out.

"Teddy! Enid! What's going on?" she shrieked.

"Enid saved my life," Teddy cried, wiping the water off his face.

"Enid," Elizabeth said wonderingly, "how did you—?"

Enid stood in the shallow end, her beautiful green eyes shining. "I don't know, Liz," she whispered. "When I saw Teddy drowning, I was out of the chair like a bolt of lightning. I didn't even stop to think, I just ran!"

"Ran!" Elizabeth gasped, jumping into the water and throwing her arms around her friend. "Oh, Enid—"

Then the three of them bounced up and down in the water, hugging one other— Enid still fully dressed, her clothes sticking to her, and Elizabeth and Teddy in their bathing suits.

"I hate to ask stupid questions," a wry voice said, "but *what* is going on around here?"

"Oh, Jess," Elizabeth cried, her face wet with water and tears, "Enid's cured! She saved Teddy's life. She jumped out of the wheelchair and walked!"

"Enid!" Jessica exclaimed. "That's wonderful!"

"Now, tell me what happened," Jessica asked after she'd brought Enid a towel.

"Well, Liz asked me to watch Teddy while she went inside to get some sodas," Enid said, wiping her streaming face. "And the next thing I knew he was in the water. Liz had just finished telling me Teddy couldn't swim, and there he was—five feet over his head! And that was the last thing I remember. I guess I just headed for the pool. And even though my legs felt wobbly, I made it!"

"Wait a minute." Jessica said. "Liz told you Teddy doesn't know how to swim?"

"Well, yes," Enid said, confused. "And he obviously couldn't. He—"

"What's going on here?" Jessica demanded.

"Teddy swims like a fish! For a six-year-old, he's amazing. And anyway—"

Enid's mouth dropped open. She looked first at Elizabeth and than at Teddy. "Do you mean—"

"I'm sorry, Enid," Elizabeth said gently. "I didn't mean to trick you. But I couldn't think of any other way!"

"Wait a minute," Enid said slowly. "I think I'd better sit down."

"You've been sitting far too long," Elizabeth told her. "That's the whole point, Enid. We had to do something!"

Enid shook her head in disbelief. "Then Dr. MacGregor was right," she said painfully. "I *could* walk all the time, and I just wouldn't let myself!"

"Enid, are you mad?" Teddy asked seriously. "I didn't mean to fake drowning. But I wanted to help Liz!"

"Of course I'm not mad!" Enid cried. "This is the happiest day of my life!"

"Oh, Enid." Elizabeth sighed and hugged the girl again. "Thank goodness you're OK again. I've been so *worried* about you—"

Enid looked down at her legs in disbelief. "It's hard to believe," she said wonderingly. "The mind is such a strange thing. I really thought I couldn't move, and there was nothing the matter with my legs at all."

"You've been through a lot, Enid," Elizabeth

said sympathetically. "But somehow it looks like the worst of it is over now."

"I think it is," Enid said slowly. "Liz, Teddy, I don't know how to thank you guys enough. And you know what I think I'm going to do now?"

"What?" Teddy asked.

"If one of you will give me a ride home," Enid announced, "I'm going to walk up to my front door. I can just imagine the look on my mother's face!"

"I think we'd better get you some dry clothes first." Jessica giggled. "No offense, Enid, but I think you'd scare your mother now!"

"What do we do with this thing?" Elizabeth wondered aloud, looking at Enid's wheelchair.

Enid shuddered. "Drown it!" she suggested. "I never want to see it again as long as I live!"

"I'll take you home," Elizabeth said when she'd given Enid some dry clothes upstairs. "Jess and I have round-the-clock Fiat privileges these days. And I can stay with you if you don't want to be alone."

Enid shook her head. "I *need* to be alone, Liz, I've got a lot to think about," she said soberly. "I think I've been denying more than just the fact that I was really all better."

"What do you mean?" Elizabeth asked carefully.

"Well, it has to do with George," Enid said slowly. "You see, Liz, I think George is really in love with Robin Wilson now. I've been trying to hang onto him, and that isn't fair. I'm going to miss him like crazy, but I really want what's best for him."

"You mean you're going to tell him it's all over?" Elizabeth asked gently.

Enid smiled painfully. "I think so," she said. "As soon as I get my courage up, that is. That's why I need some time to think."

"Well, you think, then," Elizabeth told her. "But if you need me for anything, be sure to call me."

"I'll call you no matter what," Enid promised. "And Liz—"

"Yes, Enid?"

"Thank you," Enid said, her eyes filling up with tears, "You're the best friend anyone could have."

"Oh, Enid," Elizabeth cried, throwing her arms around the girl. She felt as if an enormous burden had been lifted from her shoulders. And from the look on Enid's face, she could tell her friend felt exactly the same way.

"I don't know how word gets around so fast in Sweet Valley!" Elizabeth said, giggling. She was standing with Todd in the parking lot of the Dairi Burger, the popular humburger place downtown. "It only happened a few hours ago," she added, "and somehow everyone knows about it already!"

She and Todd had dropped into the Dairi Burger for something to eat on their way back home from the movies. It was Friday evening, and the place was packed. Elizabeth couldn't get over the reaction when she and Todd had walked inside. The whole place had gone wild! Olivia Davidson had jumped to her feet, giving Elizabeth a standing ovation. And one by one everybody else had followed suit. Jessica had been the loudest of all. "I'm so proud of you, Liz," she had declared. And Elizabeth could tell that her twin meant it.

"You're a hero, that's all," Todd said happily, giving her a warm kiss. "What you did this afternoon was nothing short of a stroke of genius!"

"Enid is the one who really deserves the credit," Elizabeth insisted. "She was so brave, Todd. I wish you could have been there!"

"I do, too," Todd told her. "But right now I think you and I need to get away from this crowd. What do you say we drive back to your house and have a midnight swim—just the two of us!"

"As long as you promise not to drown." Elizabeth giggled. "I've had enough heroism for one day, thank you very much."

As they drove back to the Wakefields' house, Elizabeth snuggled next to Todd and told him what Enid had said about George and Robin. "I really admire her," she said thoughtfully. "She's got a lot of guts, Todd. It's going to be pretty hard for her to let George go."

"She might not," Todd warned her. "Don't expect too much from her, Liz."

"No, I think she's through with pretending," Elizabeth insisted. "She called me when she got home and said she was going to see George tonight. And something tells me tonight is going to be their last date."

"We'll see," Todd said, tightening his arm around Elizabeth. "Just don't *you* go getting dumb ideas like that in your head," he admonished. "If tonight were *our* last date, I don't know what I'd do!"

"Don't worry," Elizabeth said softly, turning her head so she could kiss his cheek. "I think you're stuck with me for a long, long time."

"Good," Todd murmured happily, turning his car into the Wakefields' driveway. "Let's keep it that way!"

But if Todd had hoped for a quiet evening in the Wakefield house, he was disappointed. The split-level home was flooded with lights, and Mr. and Mrs. Wakefield came running outside to meet them as Todd turned off the engine.

"Bayside was marvelous!" Mrs. Wakefield exclaimed, giving her daughter a hug. "We had the most wonderful time, Liz. And we ran into Roger Collins! He was with your French teacher. What's her name again?"

"Ms. Dalton?" Elizabeth asked.

"Right! And Mr. Collins told us all about what you and Teddy did this afternoon. Oh, honey, I'm so proud of you! What a wonderful idea!"

"So much for a private swim." Elizabeth

sighed and squeezed Todd's hand as they followed her parents inside.

"A small price to pay for being in love with a heroine," Todd said cheerfully, sneaking in a quick kiss before they got inside.

"I think this calls for some champagne!" Mr. Wakefield was exclaiming, hurrying to the kitchen. He had put a bottle in the refrigerator earlier for the anniversary celebration.

"To your anniversary," Todd proposed, lifting his glass several minutes later.

"And to a very special daughter," Mr. Wakefield added, taking a small sip of wine.

Elizabeth's eyes filled with tears as she tasted the champagne. *I'm so lucky*, she told herself. *I have the most wonderful parents in the world, and I have Todd.*

Elizabeth just hoped that Enid would soon be as happy as she was that night. However hard it might have been to say goodbye to George, she hoped her friend would see it as a beginning, not an end.

Fourteen

"OK," Elizabeth said, propping herself up on her elbows on the sand. "Now tell me the whole thing from the beginning."

It was Saturday afternoon, and Elizabeth and Enid were at the beach, the sun warming the backs of their legs as they listened to the surf pounding the shore.

"It wasn't so bad," Enid said thoughtfully. "We actually had a pretty good time together. We were going to go to a movie, but when George came to pick me up, I told him I wanted to talk. So we went up to Miller's Point."

"Was he surprised to see you out of the wheelchair?"

"You're not kidding!" Enid laughed. "And he was so happy for me, Liz. Anyway, we talked for *hours*. He told me all about Robin. He said he had tried not to fall in love with her, but he just couldn't help it. After the accident they didn't see each other at all—not until the dance. You

146

know, I felt kind of sorry for him when he was telling me this. I was trying to imagine how I'd feel if I were in his place. And it seemed awful!"

"So then what?" Elizabeth prompted.

"Well, he told me that Robin had refused to see him until I was all better. He admitted that he wanted to go to her sooner, but she wouldn't let him. So I guess I can't even be mad at her!"

"Do you feel angry?" Elizabeth asked gently.

Enid shook her head. "That's the funny thing, Liz. I don't. I guess these things just sort of happen sometimes. And the truth of the matter is that I was trying to hang onto George because I was scared. I knew he wasn't happy with me any longer, but I couldn't bear to admit that I might be losing him. I made things really hard for him—and I told him last night how sorry I was."

"You're so wonderful, Enid!" Elizabeth told her. "George is lucky to have you for a friend."

"Well, we may not really be friends for a while," Enid admitted. "Whatever I say now, I know it's still going to hurt when I see him with Robin. But I know now that I'll get over it. It just isn't the end of the world!"

"Whatever happened to the investigation the Federal Aviation Administration was doing?" Elizabeth asked. "Did they find what caused the crash?"

"You mean I forgot to tell you? Liz, it turns out it wasn't George's fault at all. The rental plane had something faulty with the engine. It would have stalled out no matter what George did!"

147

"George must be relieved," Elizabeth commented. "Do you think he'll fly again now?"

"I don't know," Enid said thoughtfully. "He says he doesn't think so, but I hope he gets over it. Maybe it's a little like love." She giggled. "Just because you crash once doesn't mean you'll never soar again!"

Elizabeth laughed. "Enid, there may be a future for you as a writer. Did you ever think about working for a Chinese fortune-cookie company?"

"Oh!" Enid laughed and playfully showered Elizabeth with sand.

"Here comes Todd, and it looks like he's got a cooler with him!" Elizabeth said, shading her eyes with her hand.

"Thank goodness," Enid said. "I was ready to die of thirst out here."

"Is it me you want, or my soda?" Todd demanded as Elizabeth and Enid jumped up and almost knocked him over.

"Your soda!" the two girls yelled in unison, dissolving in laughter on the sand when they saw Todd's hurt expression.

I have a feeling, Elizabeth thought happily, *that everything is going to be just fine for Enid. And I haven't the tiniest doubt that it won't be long before she gets over George!*

"I don't suppose I could convince you to help me barbecue hamburgers tonight?" Mr. Wakefield asked Jessica, who was on a lounge chair filing her nails with an emery board. Elizabeth was sitting next to her, engrossed in a book.

"No, thanks," Jessica said listlessly.

"They're not still gauche, are they?" her father teased her.

Jessica raised her eyebrows and didn't say a word. *What a family*, she thought. A person couldn't even mind her own business and try to give herself a manicure without being picked on.

"How close are we to dinner?" Mrs. Wakefield asked, coming out onto the patio with trays.

"Ages and ages away," Mr. Wakefield said cheerfully.

"What's wrong, Jess? You look positively miserable," Mrs. Wakefield observed.

"Why should I be miserable?" Jessica demanded. "Just because everything I do these days seems to end up a complete disaster? I can't do *anything* right."

"Somebody around here," Mr. Wakefield observed, "is working herself into a real snit, it seems to me."

"Ned," Mrs. Wakefield said warningly. "Liz, tell us what Enid decided to do about George."

"They've broken up," Elizabeth announced. "But Enid managed to talk to George with no hard feelings."

"I *still* say he's a selfish slob." Jessica sighed.

"I don't think so, Jess," Elizabeth said mildly. "And it turns out that George and Robin really weren't seeing each other after the accident."

"Oh, yeah? What was George's car doing in front of Robin's house, then? Lila saw it too," Jessica pointed out.

"Well, George *did* go over to Robin's house just that once. But he never saw her. And he was only dropping by to tell her that he thought they shouldn't see each other any more—not until Enid was better."

"Oh," Jessica said, her cheeks reddening.

"You see, Jess, " Mr. Wakefield said mildly, "how dangerous it can be to make judgments based on circumstantial evidence. Now had this been a *real* slander case—"

Jessica leaped to her feet, her eyes blazing. She couldn't believe her father was lecturing her again! And what did she care about court cases and circumstantial evidence?

"All you guys do lately is pick on me," she said angrily. "If *Liz* had said that George was seeing Robin, you'd think she was being sensible and fair! But just because it's me, you think I'm being a flake! Well, I'm sick of always being wrong. I'm—"

"Jessica," her father said calmly, "I didn't mean to upset you. I was only—"

"Well, I *am* upset!" Jessica told him. "And I don't want hamburgers for dinner, either. If you guys will excuse me, I'm going up to my room!"

"Liz, let her go," Jessica heard her mother saying. "She'll cool down in a few minutes."

I will not, Jessica thought furiously, racing upstairs and slamming the door to her room as hard as she could. She'd had just about enough of her family treating her badly.

And since her plan to impress them had been such a miserable failure, she was going to have to come up with some other way of changing their minds about her.

Only I'd better think of something fast, she told herself, tears trickling down her cheeks as she threw herself onto her bed. *Because I don't think I can stand things the way they are around here for another minute!*

Jessica embarks on a desperate course of action in Sweet Valley High #21, RUNAWAY.

A LETTER TO THE READER

Dear Friend,

   Ever since I created the series, SWEET VALLEY HIGH, I've been thinking about a love trilogy, a miniseries revolving around one very special girl, a character similar in some ways to Jessica Wakefield, but even more devastating—more beautiful, more charming, and much more devious.

   Her name is Caitlin Ryan, and with her long black hair, her magnificent blue eyes and ivory complexion, she's the most popular girl at the exclusive boarding school she attends in Virginia. On the surface her life seems perfect. She has it all: great wealth, talent, intelligence, and the dazzle to charm every boy in the school. But deep inside there's a secret need that haunts her life.

   Caitlin's mother died in childbirth, and her father abandoned her immediately after she was born. At least that's the lie she has been told by her enormously rich grandmother, the cold and powerful matriarch who has raised Caitlin and given her everything money can buy. But not love.

   Caitlin dances from boy to boy, never staying long, often breaking hearts, yet she's so sparkling and delightful that everyone forgives her. No one can resist her.

   No one that is, but Jed Michaels. He's the new boy in school—tall, wonderfully handsome, and very, very nice. And Caitlin means to have him.

   But somehow the old tricks don't work; she can't

seem to manipulate him. Impossible! There has never been anyone that the beautiful and terrible Caitlin couldn't have. And now she wants Jed Michaels—no matter who gets hurt or what she has to do to get him.

So many of you follow my SWEET VALLEY HIGH series that I know you'll find it fascinating to read what happens when love comes into the life of this spoiled and selfish beauty—the indomitable Caitlin Ryan.

Thanks for being there, and keep reading,

Francine Pascal

A special preview of the exciting
opening chapter of the first book
in the fabulous new trilogy:

CAITLIN

BOOK ONE

LOVING

---

by Francine Pascal,
creator of the best-selling
SWEET VALLEY HIGH series

"That's not a bad idea, Tenny," Caitlin said as she reached for a book from her locker. "Actually, it's pretty good."

"You really like it?" Tenny Sears hung on every word the beautiful Caitlin Ryan said. It was the petite freshman's dream to be accepted into the elite group the tall, dark-haired junior led at Highgate Academy. She was ready to do anything to belong.

Caitlin looked around and noticed the group of five girls who had begun to walk their way, and she lowered her voice conspiratorially. "Let me think it over, and I'll get back to you later. Meanwhile let's just keep it between us, okay?"

"Absolutely." Tenny struggled to keep her excitement down to a whisper. The most important girl in the whole school liked her idea. "Cross my heart," she promised. "I won't breathe a word to anyone."

Tenny would have loved to continue the conversation, but at just that moment Caitlin remembered she'd left her gold pen in French class. Tenny was only too happy to race to fetch it.

The minute the younger girl was out of sight, Caitlin gathered the other girls around her.

"Hey, you guys, I just had a great idea for this year's benefit night. Want to hear it?"

Of course they wanted to hear what she had to say about the benefit, the profits of which would go to the scholarship fund for miners' children. Everyone was always interested in anything Caitlin Ryan had to say. She waited until all eyes were on her, then hesitated for an instant, increasing the dramatic impact of her words.

"How about a male beauty contest?"

"A what?" Morgan Conway exclaimed.

"A male beauty contest," Caitlin answered, completely unruffled. "With all the guys dressing up in crazy outfits. It'd be a sellout!"

Most of the girls looked at Caitlin as if she'd suddenly gone crazy, but Dorothy Raite, a sleek, blond newcomer to Highgate, stepped closer to Caitlin's locker. "I think it's a great idea!"

"Thanks, Dorothy," Caitlin said, smiling modestly.

"I don't know." Morgan was doubtful. "How are you going to get the guys to go along with this? I can't quite picture Roger Wake parading around on stage in a swimsuit."

"He'll be the first contestant to sign up when I get done talking to him." Caitlin's tone was slyly smug.

"And all the other guys?"

"They'll follow along." Caitlin placed the last of her books in her knapsack, zipped it shut, then gracefully slung it over her shoulder. "Everybody who's anybody in this school will just shrivel up and die if they can't be part of it. Believe me, I wouldn't let the student council down. After all, I've got my new presidency to live up to."

Morgan frowned. "I suppose." She took a chocolate bar out of her brown leather shoulder bag and began to unwrap it.

Just at that moment, Tenny came back, empty-handed and full of apologies. "Sorry, Caitlin, I asked all over, but nobody's seen it."

"That's okay. I think I left it in my room, anyway."

"Did you lose something?" Kim Verdi asked, but Caitlin dismissed the subject, saying it wasn't important.

For an instant Tenny was confused until Dorothy Raite asked her if she'd heard Caitlin's fabulous new idea for a male beauty contest. Then everything fell into place. Caitlin had sent her away in order to take credit for the idea.

It didn't even take three seconds for Tenny to make up her mind about what to do. "Sounds terrific," she said. Tenny Sears was determined to belong to this group, no matter what.

Dorothy leaned over and whispered to Caitlin. "Speaking of beauties, look who's walking over here."

Casually Caitlin glanced up at the approaching Highgate soccer star. Roger Wake's handsome face broke into a smile when he saw her. Caitlin knew he was interested in her, and up until then she'd offhandedly played with that interest—when she was in the mood.

"And look who's with him!" Dorothy's elbow nearly poked a hole in Caitlin's ribs. "Jed Michaels. Oh, my God, I've been absolutely dying to meet this guy."

Caitlin nodded, her eyes narrowing. She'd been anxious to meet Jed, too, but she didn't tell Dorothy that. Ever since his arrival as a transfer student at Highgate, Caitlin had been studying him, waiting for precisely the right moment to be introduced and to make an unforgettable impression on him. It seemed that the opportunity had just been handed to her.

"Hey, Caitlin. How're you doing?" Roger called out, completely ignoring the other girls in the group.

"Great, Roger. How about you?" Caitlin's smile couldn't have been wider. "Thought you'd be on the soccer field by now."

"I'm on my way. The coach pushed back practice half an hour today, anyway. Speaking of which, I don't remember seeing you at the last scrimmage." There was a hint of teasing in his voice.

Caitlin looked puzzled and touched her fingertips to her lips. "I was there, I'm sure—"

"We were late, Caitlin, remember?" Tenny spoke up eagerly. "I was with you at drama club, and it ran over."

"Now, how could I have forgotten? You see,

Roger"—Caitlin sent him a sly, laughing look—"we never let the team down. Jenny should know—she's one of your biggest fans."

"Tenny," the girl corrected meekly. But she was glowing from having been singled out for attention by Caitlin.

"Oh, right, Tenny. Sorry, but I'm really bad with names sometimes." Caitlin smiled at the girl with seeming sincerity, but her attention returned quickly to the two boys standing nearby.

"Caitlin," Dorothy burst in, "do you want to tell him—"

"Shhh," Caitlin put her finger to her lips. "Not yet. We haven't made all our plans."

"Tell me what?" Roger asked eagerly.

"Oh, just a little idea we have for the council fund-raiser, but it's too soon to talk about it."

"Come on." Roger was becoming intrigued. "You're not being fair, Caitlin."

She paused. "Well, since you're our star soccer player, I can tell you it's going to be the hottest happening at Highgate this fall."

"Oh, yeah? What, a party?"

"No."

"A concert?"

She shook her head, her black-lashed, blue eyes twinkling. "I'm not going to stand here and play Twenty Questions with you, Roger. But when we decide to make our plans public, you'll be the first to know. I promise."

"Guess I'll have to settle for that."

"Anyway, Roger, I promise not to let any of this other stuff interfere with my supporting the team from now on."

At her look, Roger seemed ready to melt into his Nikes.

Just at that moment Jed Michaels stepped forward. It was a casual move on his part, as though he were just leaning in a little more closely to hear the conversation. His gaze rested on Caitlin.

Although she'd deliberately given the impression of being impervious to Jed, Caitlin was acutely aware of every move he made. She'd studied him enough from a distance to know that she liked what she saw.

Six feet tall, with broad shoulders and a trim body used to exercise, Jed Michaels was the type of boy made for a girl like Caitlin. He had wavy, light brown hair, ruggedly even features, and an endearing, crooked smile. Dressed casually in a striped cotton shirt, tight cords, and western boots, Jed didn't look like the typical preppy Highgate student, and Caitlin had the feeling it was a deliberate choice. He looked like his own person.

Caitlin had been impressed before, but now that she saw him close at hand, she felt electrified. For that brief instant when his incredible green eyes had looked directly into hers, she'd felt a tingle go up her spine.

Suddenly realizing the need for an introduction, Roger put his hand on Jed's shoulder. "By the way, do you girls know Jed Michaels? He just transferred here from Montana. We've already got him signed up for the soccer team."

Immediately the girls called out a chorus of enthusiastic greetings, which Jed acknowledged with a friendly smile and a nod of his head. "Nice to meet you." Dorothy's call had been the loudest, and Jed's gaze went toward the pretty blonde.

Dorothy smiled at him warmly, and Jed grinned back. But before another word could be spoken, Caitlin riveted Jed with her most magnetic look.

"I've seen you in the halls, Jed, and hoped you'd been made welcome." The intense fire of her deep blue eyes emphasized her words.

He looked from Dorothy to Caitlin. "Sure have."

"And how do you like Highgate?" Caitlin pressed on quickly, keeping the attention on herself.

"So far, so good." His voice was deep and soft and just slightly tinged with a western drawl.

"I'm glad." The enticing smile never left Caitlin's lips. "What school did you transfer from?"

"A small one back in Montana. You wouldn't have heard of it."

"Way out in cattle country?"

His eyes glimmered. "You've been to Montana?"

"Once. Years ago with my grandmother. It's really beautiful. All those mountains . . ."

"Yeah. Our ranch borders the Rockies."

"Ranch, huh? I'll bet you ride, then."

"Before I could walk."

"Then you'll have to try the riding here—eastern style. It's really fantastic! We're known for our hunt country in this part of Virginia."

"I'd like to try it."

"Come out with me sometime, and I'll show you the trails. I ride almost every afternoon." Caitlin drew her fingers through her long, black hair, pulling it away from her face in a way she knew was becoming, yet which seemed terribly innocent.

"Sounds like something I'd enjoy,"—Jed said, smiling—"once I get settled in."

"We're not going to give him much time for riding," Roger interrupted. "Not until after soccer season, anyway. The coach already has him singled out as first-string forward."

"We're glad you're on the team," Caitlin said. "With Roger as captain, we're going to have a great season." Caitlin glanced at Roger, who seemed flattered by her praise. Then through slightly lowered lashes, she looked directly back at Jed. "But I know it will be even better now."

Jed only smiled. "Hope I can live up to that."

Roger turned to Jed. "We've got to go."

"Fine." Jed nodded.

Caitlin noticed Dorothy, who had been silent during Jed and Caitlin's conversation. She was now staring at Jed wistfully as he and Roger headed toward the door.

Caitlin quickly leaned over to whisper, "Dorothy, did you notice the way Roger was looking at you?"

Her attention instantly diverted, Dorothy looked away from Jed to look at Caitlin. "Me?" She sounded surprised.

"Yeah. He really seems interested."

"Oh, I don't think so." Despite her attraction to Jed, Dorothy seemed flattered. "He's hardly ever looked at me before."

"You were standing behind me and probably couldn't notice, but take my word for it."

Dorothy glanced at the star soccer player's retreating back. Her expression was doubtful, but for the moment she'd forgotten her pursuit of Jed, and Caitlin took that opportunity to focus her own attention on the new boy from Montana. She knew she only had a moment more to make that unforgettable impression on him before the two boys were gone. Quickly she walked forward. Her voice was light but loud enough to carry to the girls behind her.

"We were just going in your direction, anyway," she called. "Why don't we walk along just to show you what strong supporters of the team we are?"

Looking surprised, Roger said, "That's fine by us. Right, Jed?"

"Whatever you say."

Caitlin thought he sounded pleased by the attention. Quickly, before the other girls joined them, she stepped between the two boys. Roger immediately tried to pull her hand close to his side. She wanted to swat him off, but instead, gave his hand a squeeze, then let go. She was pleased when Diana fell in step beside Roger. Turning to Jed, Caitlin smiled and said, "There must be a thousand questions you still have about the school and the area. Have you been to Virginia before?"

"A few times. I've seen a little of the countryside."

"And you like it?"

As they walked out the door of the building, Jed turned his head so that he could look down into her upturned face and nodded. There was a bright twinkle in his eyes.

Caitlin took that twinkle as encouragement, and her own eyes grew brighter. "So much goes on around here at this time of year. Has anyone told you about the fall dance this weekend?"

"I think Matt Jenks did. I'm rooming with him."

"It'll be great—a real good band," Caitlin cooed. In the background she heard the sound of the others' voices, but they didn't matter. Jed Michaels was listening to *her*.

They walked together for only another minute, down the brick footpath that connected the classroom buildings to the rest of the elegant campus. Caitlin told him all she could about the upcoming dance, stopping short of asking him to be her date. She wasn't going to throw herself at him. She wouldn't have to, anyway. She knew it would be only a matter of time before he would be hers.

It didn't take them long to reach the turnoff for the soccer field. "I guess this is where I get off," she said lightly. "See you around."

"See you soon," he answered and left.

Caitlin smiled to herself. This handsome boy from Montana wasn't going to be an easy mark, but this was an adequate beginning. She wanted him—and what Caitlin wanted, Caitlin got.

"You going back to the dorm, Caitlin?" Morgan asked.

"Yeah, I've got a ton of reading to do for English lit." Caitlin spoke easily, but her thoughts were on the smile Jed Michaels had given her just before he'd left.

"Somerson really piled it on tonight, didn't she?" Gloria Parks muttered.

"Who cares about homework," Caitlin replied. "I want to hear what you guys think of Jed."

"Not bad at all." Tenny giggled.

"We ought to be asking *you*, Caitlin," Morgan added. "You got all his attention."

Caitlin brought her thoughts back to the present and laughed. "Did I? I hadn't even noticed," she said coyly.

"At least Roger's got some competition now," Jessica Stark, a usually quiet redhead, remarked. "He was really getting *unbearable*."

"There's probably a lot more to Roger than meets the eye," Dorothy said in his defense.

"I agree. Roger's not bad. And what do you expect," Caitlin added, "when all he hears is how he's the school star."

The girls started crossing the lawns from the grouping of Highgate classroom buildings toward the dorms. The magnificent grounds of the exclusive boarding school were spread out around them. The ivy-covered walls of the original school building had changed little in the two hundred years since it had been constructed as the manor house for a prosperous plantation. A sweeping carpet of lawn had replaced the tilled fields of the past; and the smaller buildings had been converted into dormitories and staff quarters. The horse stable had been expanded, and several structures had been added—classroom buildings, a gymnasium complete with an indoor pool, tennis and racketball courts—but the architecture of the new buildings blended in well with that of the old.

"Caitlin, isn't that your grandmother's car in the visitors' parking lot?" Morgan pointed toward the graveled parking area off the oak-shaded main drive. A sleek, silver Mercedes sports coupe was gleaming in the sunlight there.

"So it is." Caitlin frowned momentarily. "Wonder what she's doing here? I must have left something at the house last time I was home for the weekend."

"My dream car!" Gloria exclaimed, holding one hand up to adjust her glasses. "I've told Daddy he absolutely *must* buy me one for my sixteenth birthday."

"And what did he say?" Jessica asked.

Gloria made a face. "That I had to settle for his three-year-old Datsun or get a bicycle."

"Beats walking," Morgan said, reaching into her bag for another candy bar.

"But I'm dying to have a car like your grandmother's."

"It's not bad." Caitlin glanced up at the car. "She has the Bentley, too, but this is the car she uses when she wants to drive herself instead of being chauffeured."

"Think she'll let you bring it here for your senior year?"

Caitlin shrugged and mimicked her grandmother's cultured tones. " 'It's not wise to spoil one.' Besides, I've always preferred Jaguars."

Caitlin paused on the brick path, and the other girls stopped beside her. "You know, I really should go say hello to my grandmother. She's probably waiting for me." She turned quickly to the others. "We've got to have a meeting for this fundraiser. How about tonight—my room, at seven?"

"Sure."

"Great."

"Darn, I've got to study for an exam tomorrow," Jessica grumbled, "but let me know what you decide."

"Me, too," Kim commented. "I was on the courts all afternoon yesterday practicing for Sunday's tennis tournament and really got behind with my studying."

"Okay, we'll fill you guys in, but make sure you come to the next meeting. And I don't want any excuses. If you miss the meeting, you're out!" Caitlin stressed firmly. "I'll catch the rest of you later, then."

All the girls walked away except Dorothy, who lingered behind. Just then, a tall, elegantly dressed, silver-haired woman walked briskly down the stairs from the administrative office in the main school building. She moved directly toward the Mercedes, quickly opened the driver's door, and slid in behind the wheel.

Caitlin's arm shot up in greeting, but Regina Ryan

never glanced her way. Instead, she started the engine and immediately swung out of the parking area and down the curving drive.

For an instant Caitlin stopped in her tracks. Then with a wide, carefree smile, she turned back to Dorothy and laughed. "I just remembered. She called last night and said she was dropping off my allowance money but would be in a hurry and couldn't stay. My memory really *is* bad. I'll run over and pick it up now."

As Caitlin turned, Dorothy lightly grabbed Caitlin's elbow and spoke softly. "I know you're in a hurry, but can I talk to you for a second, Caitlin? Did you mean what you said about Roger? Was he really looking at me?"

"I told you he was," Caitlin said impatiently, anxious to get Dorothy out of the picture. "Would I lie to you?"

"Oh, no. It's just that when I went over to talk to him, he didn't seem that interested. He was more interested in listening to what you and Jed were saying."

"Roger's just nosy."

"Well, I wondered. You know, I haven't had any dates since I transferred—"

"Dorothy! You're worried about dates? Are you crazy?" Caitlin grinned broadly. "And as far as Roger goes, wait and see. Believe me." She gave a breezy wave. "I've got to go."

"Yeah, okay. And, thanks, Caitlin."

"Anytime."

Without a backward glance, Caitlin walked quickly to the administration office. The story about her allowance had been a fabrication. Regina Ryan had given Caitlin more than enough spending money when she'd been home two weeks earlier, but it would be all over campus in a minute if the girls thought there was anything marring Caitlin's seemingly perfect life.

Running up the steps and across the main marble-floored lobby that had once been the elegant entrance hall of the plantation house, she walked quickly into the dean's office and smiled warmly at Mrs. Forbes, the dean's secretary.

"Hi, Mrs. Forbes."

"Hello, Caitlin. Can I help you?"

"I came to pick up the message my grandmother just left."

"Message?" Mrs. Forbes frowned.

"Yes." Caitlin continued to look cheerful. "I just saw her leaving and figured she was in a hurry and left a message for me here."

"No, she just met on some school board business briefly with Dean Fleming."

"She didn't leave anything for me?"

"I can check with the part-time girl if you like."

"Thanks." Caitlin's smile had faded, but she waited as Mrs. Forbes stepped into a small room at the rear.

She returned in a second, shaking her head. "Sorry, Caitlin."

Caitlin forced herself to smile. "No problem, Mrs. Forbes. It wasn't important, anyway. She'll probably be on the phone with me ten times tonight."

As Caitlin hurried from the main building and set out again toward the dorm, her beautiful face was grim. Why was she always trying to fool herself? She knew there was no chance her grandmother would call just to say hello. But nobody would ever know that: She would make certain of it. Not Mrs. Forbes, or any of the kids; not even her roommate, Ginny. Not anyone!

Like it so far? Want to read more? LOVING will be available in May 1985.* It will be on sale wherever Bantam paperbacks are sold. The other two books in the trilogy, LOVE DENIED and TRUE LOVE, will also be published in 1985.

*Outside the United States and Canada, books will be available approximately three months later. Check with your local bookseller for further details.

☐	26741	**DOUBLE LOVE #1**	$2.75
☐	26621	**SECRETS #2**	$2.75
☐	26627	**PLAYING WITH FIRE #3**	$2.75
☐	26746	**POWER PLAY #4**	$2.75
☐	26742	**ALL NIGHT LONG #5**	$2.75
☐	26813	**DANGEROUS LOVE #6**	$2.75
☐	26622	**DEAR SISTER #7**	$2.75
☐	26744	**HEARTBREAKER #8**	$2.75
☐	26626	**RACING HEARTS #9**	$2.75
☐	26620	**WRONG KIND OF GIRL #10**	$2.75
☐	26824	**TOO GOOD TO BE TRUE #11**	$2.75
☐	26688	**WHEN LOVE DIES #12**	$2.75
☐	26619	**KIDNAPPED #13**	$2.75
☐	26764	**DECEPTIONS #14**	$2.75
☐	26765	**PROMISES #15**	$2.75
☐	26740	**RAGS TO RICHES #16**	$2.75
☐	26883	**LOVE LETTERS #17**	$2.75
☐	26687	**HEAD OVER HEELS #18**	$2.75
☐	26823	**SHOWDOWN #19**	$2.75
☐	26959	**CRASH LANDING! #20**	$2.75

Prices and availability subject to change without notice.

Buy them at your local bookstore or use this convenient coupon for ordering:

Bantam Books, Inc., Dept. SVH, 414 East Golf Road, Des Plaines, Ill. 60016

Please send me the books I have checked above. I am enclosing $_____
(please add $1.50 to cover postage and handling). Send check or money order
—no cash or C.O.D.s please.

Mr/Ms _____

Address _____

City/State _____ Zip _____

SVH—6/87
Please allow four to six weeks for delivery. This offer expires 12/87.

Special Offer
Buy a Bantam Book
for only 50¢.

Now you can order the exciting books you've been wanting to read straight from Bantam's latest listing of hundreds of titles. *And* this special offer gives you the opportunity to purchase a Bantam book for only 50¢. Here's how:

By ordering any five books at the regular price per order, you can also choose any other single book listed (up to $4.95 value) for only 50¢. Some restrictions do apply, so for further details send for Bantam's listing of titles today.

Just send us your name and address and we'll send you Bantam Book's SHOP AT HOME CATALOG!

BANTAM BOOKS, INC.
P.O. Box 1006, South Holland, ILL. 60473

Mr./Mrs./Miss/Ms. _____
(please print)

Address _____

City_____ State _____ Zip _____

FC(B)—11/85

Printed in the U.S.A.